D1083818

PATRIOTS IN PETTICOATS

Other Books by the Author

The Corduroy Road
Tunnels of Terror

PATRIOTS
IN
PETTICOATS

Patricia Edwards Clyne

Illustrated by Richard Lebenson

DODD, MEAD & COMPANY
New York

Library of Congress Cataloging in Publication Data

Clyne, Patricia Edwards.
    Patriots in petticoats.

    Includes index.
    SUMMARY: More than eighteen brief biographies of
women who fought for their country's independence.
Includes information on related historic sites and
markers that can be visited today.
    1. Women—United States—History—Biography—
Juvenile literature. 2. United States—History—
Revolution, 1775–1783—Juvenile literature.
[1. United States—History—Revolution, 1775–1783—
Biography] I. Lebenson, Richard. II. Title.
HQ1416.C57   973.3'092'2 [B] [920]   75–38361

ISBN 0–396–07292–5

Dedicated
to
Mernie,
a very special kind
of patriot

Contents

Introduction

Although the Revolution is generally looked upon as the war which won our independence, by no means did it settle our differences with England, and the War of 1812 was inevitable. Because it took both of these wars to fully establish our nationhood, the period covered in *Patriots in Petticoats* is from 1774 to 1814.

During those years, a variety of names were used to denote the combatants. "Redcoats" were, of course, British soldiers, whereas "Tories" or "Loyalists" meant those colonists still loyal to the crown. German soldiers hired to fight on the side of England were called "mercenaries" or "Hessians."

There were also certain outlaws who pretended to be loyal to one side or the other but whose sole interest was in lining their pockets with gold. Those who said they were pro-British were called "cowboys," while the ones who professed loyalty to the Americans were known as "skinners."

As for the colonists, they referred to themselves as "Patriots," but the British thought of them as "Rebels." They were also called "Liberty Boys" or "Whigs."

Even more varied than these names are the exploits of the women who helped to establish and maintain our country during those tumultuous years. Yet, with few exceptions, history has tended to ignore them.

Why is this so? Aside from the fact that stories may become lost with the passage of years, the attitude toward women at that time is partly to blame. Generally, women were considered to be the "keepers of the home"—domesticated beings who did not participate in the outside world of men. When they did, they were usually looked upon as oddities, and their stories often went unrecorded for many years. In fact, Nancy Hart's many exploits were not written down until half a century after they occurred.

Secrecy also played a part in keeping some stories from the public eye, and if it hadn't been for a faded valentine found many years after it was received, the full details of Sally Townsend's sacrifice might never have been known.

Another reason for the lack of attention given to the deeds of female patriots is that they seldom fought in an official capacity. (Deborah Sampson is probably the only woman who was an enlisted soldier—and then under the assumed name of "Robert Shurtleff.") Therefore, their names did not appear in public records unless they were accorded special recognition by the government, such as Mary Hays ("Molly Pitcher") and Margaret Corbin. And even when such recognition was given, the details of the heroine's act sometimes went unrecorded as in the case of Anna Maria Lane.

It is also true that many of the acts of bravery recorded here were single incidents—the reaction of ordinary women who, when faced with danger, handled desperate situations with amazing resourcefulness. Then, after the danger had passed, they returned to their everyday lives (as did Hannah Hendee) without thought that their actions were of historical significance.

The important thing, though, is that the stories which have survived should be told, and that the various sites pertaining to these heroines be recorded for those who wish to visit them. (Such sites, including directions and other pertinent information, are listed at the end of chapters.) For Americans can well be proud of the women of all ages—from eleven-year-old Phebe Reynolds to matronly Lydia Darragh—who helped to achieve our country's independence. It is for this reason *Patriots in Petticoats* has been written.

"*Mad Anne*" *Bailey*

WHITE SQUAW OF THE KANAWHA

They had expected her to cry. They had even told her it would help if she did cry. But there had been no tears in Anne's eyes when she saw the blood-drenched corpse of her husband Richard. And there were no tears in her eyes now as she walked up the frost-hardened path to the home of Mrs. Moses Mann.

As she waited for her neighbor to answer the door, Anne looked down at her seven-year-old son William. She had tried to explain what she was going to do, but she didn't think William understood.

Mrs. Mann didn't understand either. This was obvious from what she said as soon as Anne revealed her plan.

"I think Richard's death has affected your judgment," Mrs. Mann told her. "There were other men besides Richard killed at the Battle of Point Pleasant. You don't see their widows dressed in buckskin and riding all over

1

the countryside. They accept their loss and wear their black dresses in the proper . . ."

"A widow's weeds will not ease my grief," Anne broke in. "As for accepting Richard's death, I can only do that if I go on this mission."

Mrs. Mann got up from her chair by the fire to hand Anne's son a bucket. "Fetch us some water from the stream, William," she requested.

Once the boy was beyond the sound of their voices, Mrs. Mann turned again to Anne. "Recruiting volunteers to serve in the militia is a noble cause, but one that is best left to men. Riding alone on the frontier is too dangerous for a woman, Anne. William has already lost his father. Do you want him to lose his mother too?"

Anne did not answer her friend's question. Instead, she asked, "Will you care for William while I am away?"

"You must not abandon him, Anne!" Mrs. Mann said sternly.

"I have no intention of abandoning my only son," Anne stated just as sternly. "I only want to help make the frontier safe, so that William won't die as his father did—tortured to death by Indians! Now, will you take care of him for me?"

Mrs. Mann nodded slowly. "You know I will, Anne."

A few minutes later, Anne said good-bye to her son and started down the path to her own cabin.

"Mother!"

The boy's plaintive cry halted her steps momentarily. "Don't you worry, William," she called. "I'll be back. I promise you that!"

On that day in October, 1774, Anne Bailey began a life that was to make her a legend on the western frontier of Virginia. Wearing a hunting shirt atop buckskin leggings and carrying a long rifle, she tirelessly rode from one settlement to another, recruiting soldiers to fight the Indians—and the British. For the Battle of Point Pleasant (which historians now call the first battle of the Revolution) made it apparent that the colonies would soon be fighting an all-out war to gain their independence.

The lone figure on horseback became a familiar sight throughout the Kanawha Valley. She was welcomed by soldier and settler alike, for in addition to her many other talents, Anne was a skilled nurse who gave freely of her time and attention.

During the Revolutionary War Anne acted as a scout and messenger, fearlessly traveling through enemy territory to bring vital information to distant outposts. Anne's courage was not based on recklessness, however. Not only was she an excellent marksman, but she knew as much about wilderness survival as any Indian.

When she was ready to make camp, Anne would ride

about a half mile past the site she had selected. Then she would turn her horse loose and walk back, so that any pursuing Indians would be thrown off her trail.

Caves and hollow trees were her favorite campsites, as they offered dry storage for her ammunition. And more than once such natural shelters saved her life.

One winter she was caught in a blizzard and was unable to start a fire. Crawling into a hollow tree, she drew her horse's head close to her so that the animal's warm breath would keep her from freezing.

Another time, when she was being followed by a band of warring Indians, Anne crawled into a hollow log. The Indians continued to search for her. They even sat on the log she was hiding in, but they did not discover her. Finally, they left, taking with them her favorite horse, Liverpool.

Anne waited until nightfall, then tracked the Indians to their camp. Moving silently and unseen through the trees, she soon spotted Liverpool among the other horses. Then with a bloodcurdling cry of defiance, she leaped on Liverpool's back and galloped off to safety.

It was this act and similar ones that convinced the Indians she was insane, and they began calling her the "White Squaw of the Kanawha." To others, she was simply "Mad Anne."

No madwoman, however, could have accomplished what Anne did in 1791. Though the Revolution had

ended, there was still trouble with the Indians along the western Virginia frontier. Therefore, Anne continued to serve as a scout—this time at Fort Lee (the present site of Charleston, West Virginia).

A large body of Indians had surrounded the fort when Colonel George Clendenin discovered he was almost out of gunpowder. Assembling his men, he asked for a volunteer to ride over a hundred miles to Lewisburg and bring back the needed powder.

Not one hand was raised for what was considered to be a suicide mission.

Clendenin was about to turn away when a voice called out, "I will go!" It was Anne Bailey.

Late that night, Anne silently led her horse out of the fort. Using every trick she had ever learned, she managed to elude the Indians ringing the fort, then galloped for Lewisburg. What is more, she slipped past them again on her return journey, and delivered the powder in time to save Fort Lee from destruction.

Four years later, in 1795, the Treaty of Greenville brought peace to the Kanawha Valley. Anne was no longer needed as a scout, but she did not give up her rugged life. Instead, she became a "one-woman express agency," delivering goods needed by settlers in outlying districts. This service was especially welcomed by the wilderness farmers, who knew that Anne's cheerful "I'll be back" was a promise which could be broken only by death.

Nor did she break the promise she had made that October day in 1774. Eventually Anne did return to her son William. And it was on his farm in November, 1825, that she died peacefully in her sleep, knowing that the Kanawha Valley was now safe for all who chose to make their home there.

WHAT CAN BE SEEN TODAY

WEST VIRGINIA: The most prominent of the memorials to the "White Squaw of the Kanawha" marks her grave in Tu-Endie-Wei Park (at "The Point" where the Kanawha and Ohio rivers meet) in Point Pleasant. The adjacent Mansion Museum is open from April through November. About sixty miles to the southeast, a large boulder on Kanawha Boulevard in Charleston commemorates Anne Bailey's ride to bring powder to Fort Lee. There is also a marker to her in Watoga State Park (on Route 63) near Workman's Ridge, which Anne Bailey is said to have used as a lookout point.

VIRGINIA: Half a mile north of Byers Store in Falling Spring is Anne Bailey's Cave, believed to be her stopping-place when she was a scout. (The cave is half a mile from the road on property owned by A.A. Forbes of Covington. Visitors should first obtain permission from him.) On Route 220N, eight miles north of Covington, a marker describes where she once lived on "Mad Anne's Ridge."

Penelope Barker

THE EDENTON TEA PARTY

As she arranged the inkpot and quills on the table before her, Penelope Barker glanced out the window with a worried frown. Though it was early in the day, numerous birds were already roosting in the tree outside—a sure sign that bad weather was on its way.

"I do hope the approaching storm does not reach Edenton until after our meeting is over," she said to her hostess, Elizabeth King.

Mrs. King nodded absently as she directed a servant to place a tray of teacups on the sideboard.

"The ladies might not come if the weather is bad," Penelope persisted.

"Oh, they will come all right," Mrs. King assured her. "But whether they sign your paper may be another story. You know as well as I do that many of the people hereabouts still think of England as their home."

Penelope looked down at the paper she had set next to the inkpot. "But remember what the people of Boston did last year. They dumped a whole shipload of tea into the harbor. Then last August our own Provincial Congress voted to ban imports from England, unless those oppressive taxes are lifted."

Mrs. King was nodding again. "I know all that," she said. "But those things were done by men. What you are suggesting today concerns women, and might well be considered audacious and unladylike."

"I think the ladies of Edenton will sign my document. After all, it says that . . ." Penelope was interrupted by the sound of a carriage driving up, which forced her to delay her explanation until all the guests had arrived.

A total of fifty-one women assembled in Elizabeth King's home on that October day in 1774. And at the end of their meeting, each and every one of them had signed Penelope Barker's declaration which supported the proposed ban on English imports. They would neither drink tea from Britain nor wear clothes made of British cloth.

Penelope had been correct after all. But so was Mrs. King. When news of the "Edenton Tea Party" reached England, the reaction was immediate and intense. As one Londoner jokingly asked, "Is there a female congress in Edenton, too?"

Then on March 25, 1775, a biting cartoon appeared

in London, called "A Society of Patriotic Ladies at Edenton, North Carolina." But even this coarse attempt to make fun of a serious matter did not mask the fact that even the women of the colonies were uniting against the "Mother Country" England. What is more, unlike the Boston Tea Party, when the participants had hidden their identity under the guise of Indians, these North Carolina women had openly signed their names to the declaration drawn up by Penelope Barker.

The Edenton Tea Party was not the only occasion when Penelope demonstrated the kind of courage and determination which won the country's independence.

Several years later, when the Revolution was being fought, the British marched into Edenton. Penelope Barker's husband was not at home, but this did not deter her when she saw British soldiers lead her carriage horses from the stables. Quickly lifting her husband's sword from its place on the wall, she ran outside to confront the Redcoats.

When they refused to heed her protests, she did not hesitate to wield the heavy sword. With one stroke, she severed the reins the soldiers held. Then, without another word, she turned her back on them and led her horses into the stable.

The soldiers were about to follow her when their officer stopped them. Such bravery, he declared, could not go unrecognized, and he ordered that Penelope

Barker be allowed to keep her horses. Nor was this courageous patriot ever bothered again by the British for the duration of the war.

WHAT CAN BE SEEN TODAY

NORTH CAROLINA: Although the house where the Edenton Tea Party was held no longer exists, the site (on Courthouse Square) is marked by a large bronze teapot atop a Revolutionary cannon. The home of Penelope Barker (on South Broad Street), as well as the nearby Cupola House, where she spent a great deal of time in her later years, are open to the public every day except Monday.

The tea caddy used during the Edenton Tea Party is on display at the North Carolina Museum of History, located at 109 East Jones Street in Raleigh. (The museum is open daily.) There is also a bronze plaque commemorating the event in the Rotunda of the State Capitol, on Capitol Square (bounded by Salisbury, Morgan, Wilmington, and Edenton streets), in Raleigh. The Capitol is open to the public on weekdays.

NEW YORK: Three rooms from the Edenton Cupola House are on permanent display in the Decorative Arts Galleries of the Brooklyn Museum, which is open every day except Monday and Tuesday.

Mary Lindley Murray

HOSTESS WITH A SECRET

"Hurrah! General Howe has just landed at Kips Bay with 8,000 troops!"

Robert Murray was so delighted with his announcement, he did not notice the stricken glances that passed between his wife Mary and their daughters Beulah and Susan.

When they continued to remain silent, the wealthy New York merchant spoke again. "We must greet Howe as he passes by. Since he knows I am a staunch Loyalist, he will not mind the waves of three rebel sympathizers."

Mary Murray frowned at her husband's reference to the only thing they disagreed on. She knew it was not right for families to be divided like this. But she also knew that nothing or nobody could ever change her belief in the American cause—a cause now seriously endangered by the arrival of British General William Howe.

"I trust my three ladies will be suitably attired for welcoming General Howe and his party."

Her hubsand's words galvanized Mary into action, but she did not follow Beulah and Susan upstairs. Instead, she hurried in the direction of the kitchen, where she found one of her maids anxiously waiting.

Taking the girl into a corner of the pantry, Mary whispered, "What news of General Washington? Has he escaped?"

"He's already north of here, at Harlem Heights. The army is divided into three parts for the retreat. Generals Spencer, Greene, and Putnam are each leading a part."

"But are *they* safe?" Mary asked impatiently.

"Spencer and Greene are already on their way up the Boston Post Road, but Putnam . . ."

"What about General Putnam?"

"Word came that he is still south of here, evacuating the lower part of Manhattan. He cannot move quickly because he is transporting the army's stores and ammunition. Plus that, there are a large number of citizens evacuating with him."

Mary was silent for a few minutes. Then she said slowly, "So if Howe continues marching west from

Kips Bay, he will cut off Putnam's retreat . . . but only if he continues. *And he will have to come past here first!*"

Suddenly Mary gripped the maid's shoulder. "There may still be a way! Now listen to me carefully. Go up to the cupola and keep watch for Putnam."

"But how can I do that?" the girl protested. "The trees are so thick hereabouts, I won't be able to see which road General Putnam takes."

"You don't have to," Mary told her. "Just watch for the dust. An army that size, with so many supply wagons, will churn up a cloud of dust that will rise over the treetops. When that cloud has moved past this house, come down and tell me—but only then."

The maid had just scurried upstairs to her post at the cupola window, when a voice sounded behind Mary.

"Surely you have not forgotten you were to change your dress," Robert Murray chided.

"Indeed not," Mary told her husband. "But if you intend to offer General Howe some refreshments, then arrangements must be made."

A mixture of surprise and pleasure appeared on his face. But before he could say anything, Mary added, "I may be called a rebel sympathizer, but never a poor hostess." Then she hurried off to complete her preparations.

In New York, it is not unusual to have stifling hot days in September. And the fifteenth of that month in 1776 was one of those days.

By the time British General Howe reached Belmont, the home of Mary and Robert Murray, he was only too happy to accept their invitation to stop for a cooling drink in the spacious parlor of the mansion.

When he was sufficiently rested and was preparing to leave, Mary pointed out that it was midday and the general must surely be hungry. "Why, it will take no time at all for you to have your luncheon," she insisted charmingly.

New York Governor William Tryon, who was a Tory and had accompanied Howe from Kips Bay, urged the general to stay. After all, he pointed out, their hostess was well known for her lavish hospitality, and the day was exceedingly warm.

Howe hesitated. He had sent part of his troops south with Count Donop, but the rest of them were waiting outside in the hot sun.

"No problem, General," Mary hastily assured him, and directed his attention to a window overlooking the vast grounds surrounding Belmont. Outside, in the shade of the trees, great kegs of ale had been brought from the cellar of the mansion and set up on tables, along with food for the soldiers.

Thanking his hostess for her thoughtfulness, General

Howe agreed to enjoy the sumptuous meal waiting for him in the dining room, as well as the charming presence of the two lovely Murray daughters, Beulah and Susan.

None was more charming, though, than Mary when Howe at last said he must leave. "It is much too hot to exert yourself after a meal," Mary protested. "Perhaps a bit of wine while you wait. Robert imported a very special Madeira that you simply *must* try."

Once again the gentlemanly general found it impossible to deny the pleas of his gracious hostess. Thus, the afternoon hours passed by until finally Mary Murray saw that her maid had come down from the cupola.

While passing a tray of fruitcake to her mistress, the girl managed to whisper, "Putnam is now at least a mile north of here. He'll soon be safe at Harlem Heights."

The girl was right. Before darkness descended on New York that hot September day, General Israel Putnam reached the northern tip of Manhattan, where the rest of the American army was encamped.

And, as George McVay later said at the unveiling of a tablet commemorating the heroic lady who made this possible:

> It was ever afterward the remark of the American army that during the darkest period in the history of the Revolutionary War it was saved, and our present

independence secured, through Robert Murray's wine and the wit of his wife, Mary Lindley Murray.

WHAT CAN BE SEEN TODAY

NEW YORK: On the southwest corner of Park Avenue and 35th Street in New York City, there is a tablet marking the property once owned by Robert Murray, and mentioning his wife's "signal service in the Revolutionary War." A second plaque describing her "delaying action" is located two blocks to the north, at 37th Street and Park Avenue. (The marker is on an ivy-covered boulder behind the iron fence of the median divider, right at the crosswalk.) A painting of Mrs. Murray receiving the British officers is part of the Bicentennial exhibit, "Revolution in New York," at the Museum of the City of New York (Fifth Avenue at 103rd Street), which is open every day except Monday.

Margaret Corbin

DEFENDER OF FORT WASHINGTON

A savage November wind snarled at the couple standing on the crest of Forest Hill. The young woman shivered, but she made no move to seek shelter behind what was the northernmost redoubt of Fort Washington.

"When they attack," she said finally, "from which direction will they come?"

Before answering his wife, John Corbin looked north to where the upper tip of Manhattan Island was separated from the mainland by only a narrow strip of water.

Pointing to it in the predawn grayness, he said, "The Hessians need only cross the King's Bridge."

"Then they'll attack from the north?" Margaret Corbin asked.

John nodded. "Aye, from the north." Then he turned to his right. Across the Harlem River, hundreds of campfires flickered like fireflies in the distance. "And from the east."

He made another quarter turn. "And from the south."

The heels of his heavy boots crunched ominously as he completed the circle, his left arm pointing to the Hudson River far below, where the British warship *Pearl* rode at anchor. "And even from the west," he concluded grimly.

Unwilling to hear what she knew her husband would say next, Margaret walked a few yards away. But John followed, imprisoning her in a gentle but inescapable embrace.

"There is still time for you to slip away," he began. "General Washington is just across the Hudson at Fort Lee. From there, you can go back to our home in Pennsylvania."

"No, John," came her reply. "I have never left your side since we were married four years ago. I will not do so now."

There was no anger in the young man's eyes. Yet his voice was harsh when he said, "But you don't understand. The Hessians and Redcoats outnumber us at least three to one!"

"All the more reason for me to stay," Margaret countered. "Remember what Colonel Magaw said today when the British demanded that we surrender?" Then slowly, Margaret repeated the defiant words of the Pennsylvania commander:

Actuated by the most glorious cause that mankind ever fought in, I am determined to defend this post to the very last extremity.

John Corbin listened in silence. He now knew there was no chance of changing Margaret's mind—just as he knew there was no chance of the Americans winning the battle that would take place later in the day.

The British did not win easily, however. Time and again as they stormed up Forest Hill (now known as Fort Tryon), the Hessians were repulsed by the fire from the two-gun emplacement where John Corbin served as matross.

A matross only assisted in loading and sponging the cannon. Yet when the gunner in charge fell dead, John Corbin quickly took over. At his side was his wife Margaret, who now assumed the role of matross. Together they kept the cannon roaring down at the Hessian horde.

Despite the deadly fire, the Hessians continued to crawl painfully over the jagged rocks of Forest Hill. In places where they could not stand, they pulled themselves up by the aid of the birch trees growing along the slope.

All the while the cannons filled the air with a thunder that was deafening. Then suddenly one explosion seemed louder to Margaret than all the rest. Looking up from where she was stooping over their dwindling supply of gunpowder, she saw John reel back, blood spurting from a direct hit.

There was nothing she could do to help him—nothing but to take his place at the cannon.

Acting as both matross and gunner, Margaret Corbin kept her cannon firing until a charge of red-hot grapeshot tore through her upper body. Only then was her gun silent as she fell near the body of her husband.

A few minutes later, the blue-coated Hessians stormed over the barricade, their flashing bayonets ending the last resistance on Forest Hill.

Late in the afternoon of November 16, 1776, a blood-smeared doctor wearily climbed up to the now silent redoubt, searching for the wounded. He was about to turn away when he spied a slight movement near one of the cannons. Bending down, he shook his head in disbelief. What he had thought was the shattered corpse of a soldier was actually a woman—and she was alive!

Two centuries ago, the practice of medicine was comparatively primitive, with no such things as blood transfusions or penicillin. Therefore, it is amazing that Margaret Corbin survived the shower of grapeshot that lacerated her chest and jaw, and almost tore her left arm from her body.

Even more amazing is the fact that, in this condition, she endured a jolting ride of almost one hundred miles to Philadelphia. For it was there the American wounded were sent after the British victory at Fort Washington.

Nothing more was heard of Margaret Corbin until July, 1777, when Congress approved the formation of an Invalid Regiment made up of disabled soldiers. Though she had been only a volunteer nurse and aide to her husband's unit, and not an enlisted soldier, her outstanding heroism and sacrifice could not be denied. So it was that "Captain Molly," as people had begun to call her, was immediately enrolled in this regiment and assigned to West Point.

With the end of the war in 1783, the Invalid Regiment was mustered out, but Margaret Corbin was not forgotten. In time, a grateful Congress voted her a lifetime pension, for her wounds had permanently disabled her. She was the first woman ever to receive such a grant from the United States government—a fitting reward for "the first American woman to take a soldier's part in the War for Liberty."

WHAT CAN BE SEEN TODAY

NEW YORK: "Captain Molly" is buried in Section II of the United States Military Academy Cemetery at West Point, New

York. A bronze bas-relief on the granite marker depicts her heroic action at the Battle of Fort Washington. There is also a watercolor of her on display in the West Point Museum, located on Thayer Road. (The museum is open every day except Christmas and New Year's.)

In New York City's Fort Tryon Park (Broadway and 192nd Street) there is a bronze marker inscribed to her on the wall of the simulated fortifications. Another commemorative marker can be found in Holy Rood Church, Fort Washington Avenue and West 179th Street. (The park can be visited at any time; the church during Sunday morning services.)

Sybil Ludington

THE FEMALE PAUL REVERE

"Will Papa stay home this time?"

Sybil Ludington smiled as she tucked the covers around the boy. Each of her seven brothers and sisters had asked the same question at least twice since Colonel Ludington had come home from war.

"He'll be here for a while," Sybil told her youngest brother. "The men have been given only enough time to do their spring planting."

"Then Papa will have to go back again?"

"Yes, the war is far from over," she replied with a sigh. "Now, close those eyes. I must get back downstairs, for I hear a horse coming into the mill yard."

The boy listened for a moment, then said, "Maybe it's General Washington!"

"Not likely," Sybil laughed. "He's probably gone

home to Virginia to do his spring planting too. Now, no more of your delaying tactics, young man. *Good night!*"

Her brother grinned in good-natured defeat. "Night, Syb," he called, for she was already on her way downstairs.

Before she reached the large kitchen, Sybil could hear the drumlike sound of a heavy fist on the front door.

"Colonel Ludington! Colonel Ludington!" a voice cried out urgently. "The British are raiding Danbury!"

Sybil raced into the room just as the exhausted messenger was being led to a chair by the fire.

"Why, Danbury's less than thirty miles to the east!" she exclaimed. But neither of the two men even noticed her presence.

Her grim-faced father was listening intently as the messenger related that Danbury, Connecticut, had been left virtually unprotected. When the American troops were dismissed to take care of the spring planting, only 150 militiamen had remained behind to guard the storehouses of the Continental Army. This small force could do little to stem the onrushing tide of the enemy. Even now, General William Tryon's 2,000 troops were looting and burning the town.

"We must immediately recall our men from their farms!" Colonel Ludington declared. "Everyone must be warned, for the British may not stop at Danbury.

They may decide to raid here as well. We'll have the men meet here at the mill. As soon as they arrive, I . . ."

Sybil's father stopped suddenly when he realized the spent condition of the man before him. With a worried frown, he went on, "But who will summon the men? You're too exhausted to ride farther. And I must stay here to muster the men as they arrive. There is no one else who . . ."

"I can!" Sybil's voice rang out. "I will sound the alarm."

"A sixteen-year-old girl?" Colonel Ludington almost gasped, then began shaking his head negatively. "The night is dark and the roads unsafe—Tories and brigands infest every byway."

"I know all the farms. I can do it!" Sybil insisted.

"But daughter, it would be many miles—many dark and dangerous miles. I cannot permit . . ."

"Father," Sybil broke in, "the people must be warned —and there simply is no one else to do it."

Before Colonel Ludington could answer, Sybil had rushed outside to the shed where the horses were kept. Within minutes, she had slipped a bridle over her favorite horse's head. After firmly cinching the saddle, she leaped on his back.

Colonel Ludington was standing outside as she rode up. There was worry—but also a touch of pride—in his voice when he told his daughter, "Remember, the men are to muster here at the mill. Also tell the women to gather their valuables and be ready to move out at a moment's notice should Tryon get this far."

Sybil nodded as she prodded her mount with the small stick she carried. The horse's hoofs sounded like thunder on the frost-hardened ground. Soon the lights of the Ludington house were swallowed up by the dark trees that arched the road behind her.

Even though it was late April, the night was chill and Sybil was shivering by the time she reached the first farmhouse. Without dismounting, she called, "The British are burning Danbury! Muster at Colonel Ludington's mill! Prepare for a British raid!"

The startled farmer who appeared at the door did not seem to comprehend, so Sybil shouted her message again, then galloped off.

She traveled south toward Carmel, crying out her warning at each farm. Then on to Lake Mahopac. There were no lights burning in the homes now, for the hour was late. Without these small and welcoming beacons, Sybil felt her courage faltering, and she fought back the tears of fear as she rode on.

All too well she remembered the stories of the notorious "cowboys" who roamed the area. Though they professed to be helping the British, the cowboys were really only lawless murderers who plundered outlying districts for their own selfish gain.

For one swift moment, Sybil felt like turning back. But the reality of the British at Danbury was much more frightening than the possibility of meeting any cowboys, and she rode on.

The coldness of the April night had numbed her hands and feet by the time she reached Tompkins Corners, and the horse's breath was rasping. She knew it would be impossible to reach each and every home in the area, but the ones she did notify could warn the others.

Farmer's Mills was a few minutes behind her when she felt her horse falter. He was tiring now, she realized, and well he might, for they had already covered nearly thirty miles.

"Only a little while longer," she consoled the laboring animal, as well as herself.

Over and over her cry was heard, so that by the time Sybil left Pecksville on her way home, her voice was no more than a hoarse croak. But she had done it. She had warned her neighbors of the British threat!

The Ludington mill yard was full of men when Sybil guided the weary horse through the front gate. In the flurry of preparing for the march to Danbury, there was little more than a hurried "Well done, Sybil." But in quieter days, when the British had finally been driven from the land, the story of Sybil Ludington's heroic ride would be repeated with pride, and she would be remembered forever afterward as the "Female Paul Revere."

(Note: General Tryon's troops never got as far as Putnam County, New York, where Sybil Ludington made her historic midnight ride. Thanks to the prompt mustering of the militia, the British were halted at Ridgefield, Connecticut, on April 27, 1777, and were forced to retreat to their ships in Long Island Sound.)

WHAT CAN BE SEEN TODAY

NEW YORK: The midnight ride of New York's "Female Paul Revere" (commemorated on a U.S. postage stamp issued in 1975) is detailed on historic markers which dot the route she took through northeastern Putnam County. In Carmel, where Route 52 parallels the eastern shore of Lake Glenida, there is a large equestrian statue of her.

A few miles to the north along the same road is the site of the old Ludington gristmill, the starting point of Sybil's ride. (The dead-end road leading to the marked mill site is on the right-hand side of Route 52, just past the Route 84 overpass, going from Carmel.) There is an excellent one-third scale replica of the mill at the adjacent Mill Pond Nursery (open daily), where the original millstones are also on display.

A room from the old Ludington store can be seen at the Putnam County Historical Society (63 Chestnut Street, Cold Spring), as well as other items pertaining to Sybil and her family.

WASHINGTON, D.C.: In Memorial Continental Hall of the National Society of the Daughters of the American Revolution (1776 D Street, N.W.), there is a replica of the statue at Carmel, as well as a painting of the sculptor when he was working on the original. (The DAR building is open every day except Saturday, Sunday, and legal holidays.)

Lydia Darragh

SAVED BY A SACK OF FLOUR

"But what if some woman has her baby tonight?"

"Then she will have to find another midwife," Lydia Darragh told her husband, "for I cannot attend her. The messenger from General Howe said we are not to leave the house tonight. In fact, you and the children are to be in bed and asleep before the British officers arrive."

William Darragh scowled as he looked out the window. "How unfortunate that we happen to live across the street from General Howe's headquarters and they must use our house for their staff meetings."

Before answering, Lydia finished dusting the table at which the British officers would sit. "Maybe not so unfortunate," she murmured more to herself than to her husband. "Maybe not so unfortunate at all."

A few minutes after seven that night, the first of the British officers arrived. "You may be off to bed now,

Friend Darragh," he told Lydia sternly. "I will let the others in."

Understanding his words for the order they were meant to be, Lydia bid the Englishman good night and went toward her room—but not to sleep. Instead, she entered a small closet next to the room in which the officers were meeting. Pressing her ear to the wall, she listened intently as the conference got under way.

As Quakers, the Darraghs were opposed to war. Yet as Americans, they endorsed the patriot cause. And well they might, for they had come to Philadelphia from Ireland—a country which had long suffered under British domination.

However, Lydia Darragh had an even more personal reason for eavesdropping on the night of December 2, 1777. A short time before, her twenty-two-year-old son Charles had abandoned the Quaker belief in pacifism and joined the Continental Army. He was now stationed at Whitemarsh, less than two dozen miles from British-held Philadelphia.

Therefore, Lydia could not restrain a gasp when she heard the British officers mention the word "Whitemarsh." Then suddenly their voices stopped. Had they heard her gasp? Lydia held her breath, ready to race for her bedroom. But no. There was a faint rustle of paper inside the conference room; then the voices resumed.

Satisfied that they had only paused to look at a map, Lydia strained to hear whether Whitemarsh would be mentioned again.

She had not long to wait. The site of General Washington's encampment was repeated, along with such words as "surprise" and "attack." Silently, Lydia added another word—"defeat." For she knew that would be the fate of the Americans if they were surprised by the British at Whitemarsh. However, if Washington could be warned in advance . . .

The Quaker housewife was so busy with her own plans, she almost missed hearing the scrape of chairs that signaled the close of the conference. Just seconds before the door of the meeting room opened, Lydia shut her own bedroom door behind her.

Heavy boots sounded on the white oak floorboards, going toward the stairs. Then they stopped—right by her door! Had they heard her? Did they know she had been listening?

Lydia shivered when a knock sounded upon her bedroom door.

"Friend Darragh," a voice called softly.

It was not a stern command, and Lydia opened her lips to answer. Then she realized that anyone asleep— as she was supposed to be—would not readily hear such a quiet summons. So she remained silent.

The knock sounded again—this time harder. Still she did not answer.

Then when the knocking became a heavy pounding, Lydia called out in what she hoped was a sleepy-sounding voice, "Yes, what is it?"

"Sorry to awaken you, Friend Darragh," came a voice from the other side of the door. "But we are leaving now. You'd best come lock the door after us."

"I shall," she called back. "Thank you for letting me know—everything."

The British officer did not hear Lydia's last whispered word. However, he was to recall this midnight conversation two days later when the British found the Americans had been warned of the "surprise attack."

Unwilling to risk a sustained assault on Washington's troops, who were by then well prepared for the expected attack, British General Howe angrily ordered his soldiers to march back to Philadelphia.

The general had no way of knowing that his "defeat" had been caused, in part, by a small and frail Quaker housewife. Yet it was only too obvious that the secret had leaked out somehow. Then he remembered the house where the battle plans had been discussed.

When she was summoned by the British, Lydia Darragh's face turned the same color as the Quaker-gray dress she was wearing. But her voice did not betray her as she answered that her family had indeed been asleep long before the conference began.

Anxiously she awaited the next question. What if the British officer asked about *her?* Did he know that lying for any purpose was forbidden in her Quaker belief?

For long moments the officer stared at her sternly. Then, amazingly, he smiled. "I don't have to ask whether you were asleep," he said. "I well remember the difficulty I had in awakening you."

Color returned to the ashen face of Lydia Darragh and she too smiled. Her secret was secure and she had not been forced to lie about it!

This secret was kept for many years until Lydia felt it was safe to reveal it. Then she told her daughter Ann how she had set out that frigid December morning in 1777 to warn General Washington.

It was about fourteen miles from the Darragh home on South Second Street to Whitemarsh, and only those Philadelphians who had passes were allowed through the British lines. Saying she was in dire need of flour which could only be purchased from one of the mills outside the city, Lydia had succeeded in obtaining a pass.

Upon reaching Pearson's Mill in Frankford, she had left her empty flour sack to be filled. Then she had continued along the snowy road, fully determined to walk all the way to Whitemarsh if necessary.

Fortunately, her journey had been shortened by an

American colonel who was scouting the road from Philadelphia. When the exhausted and nearly frozen Lydia related her story, he took her to a nearby farmhouse to rest, while he rode on to Washington's headquarters with the news.

Lydia, however, had not been content to entrust her vital information to a single messenger. Therefore, she had rolled up a note in a small case used for carrying needles and pins. Then she had one of the farm women deliver the case to another American officer at a nearby tavern.

Finally satisfied that her mission had been successful, the resolute woman had trudged the long weary miles back to Philadelphia. Nor had she forgotten to pick up the sack of flour on her way home. After all, her need of flour had been the truth—if only part of the reason for her trek into the cold and snow-clad countryside.

WHAT CAN BE SEEN TODAY

PENNSYLVANIA: Unfortunately, there are no monuments to Lydia Darragh, but the encampment she helped to save is now Fort Washington State Park, where the old redoubts still can be seen. (Open year round, the park is located on the Bethlehem Turnpike between the towns of Fort Washington and Flourtown, Pennsylvania.) Just north of the park, also on the Bethlehem Turnpike, is Clifton House, where the Fort Washington Historical Society maintains a museum open to visitors every Thursday.

Nancy Hart

AMAZON OF WAR WOMAN'S CREEK

The southern twilight was creeping over Fort Grierson like a ghostly gray cat. The few tradespeople from Augusta who would do business with the British had already left for their homes, and the sentry was restless. His belly was rumbling with hunger, yet his relief was already ten minutes overdue.

When the sentry finally sighted him, the relief soldier was walking slowly behind a tall figure who seemed reluctant to leave the protective walls of the fort.

"I don't like the looks of him," the relief man whispered as he came up to the sentry. "He acts odd, like a . . ."

"Oh, him," the sentry interrupted. "He's just some poor madman who showed up here a few days ago. He's harmless enough."

The relief man frowned. "Maybe so, but he was most interested in what Colonel Grierson was saying to a scout. What's more, he sounds just like a woman!"

"A woman!" the sentry laughed. "Did you ever see a woman that tall? Why, he must be six feet if he's an inch! As for the voice, you know how madmen sometimes screech and squawk. But if he bothers you, I'll get rid of him before I leave."

Marching resolutely over to the tall figure shambling along, the sentry prodded him with the butt of his gun. "Move on, now!" he ordered.

The newcomer jerked back angrily. For a brief moment the hat-shaded face was revealed. There was a flash of cold blue eyes—eyes without the faintest trace of insanity. Then the madman lowered his head and shuffled off.

The sentry stared after him, gun half-raised, about to call him back. But it was suppertime and he was hungry. So with a shrug, he turned over his post to the relief man, unaware that the "madman" who had just passed through the gate was indeed a woman—the legendary Nancy Hart.

Little is known about Nancy Hart's early life, but it is not hard to imagine the teasing she must have endured because of her tremendous size. (A six-foot woman is still not too common nowadays, but two hundred years ago when people were much shorter, Nancy was considered an Amazon.)

Perhaps to compensate for this, plus her rather homely features, Nancy set out to improve whatever talents she had. Most pioneer woman knew something about nursing and herb remedies—Nancy became an expert. Frontier women usually learned how to load and fire a gun—Nancy became a sharpshooter. And, of course, women were taught how to cook—Nancy was so good, the story is still told how she could "prepare a pumpkin in as many ways as there are days in a week."

All of this did not go unnoticed by young Benjamin Hart, who had no qualms about proposing to a woman who towered high above him. The young couple was married and around 1771 they moved to northern Georgia. There Benjamin built a cabin near the bank of a small stream which would later be called War Woman's Creek.

Life was not easy in the sparsely settled country northwest of Augusta, Georgia, and the coming of the Revolutionary War made it even more difficult. Indians in the pay of the British frequently raided outlying homes, but they soon learned to stay away from the cabin where the "War Woman" lived. For more than once Nancy had proven her unerring aim with a gun—or, for that matter, with a ladle of boiling soap which she once tossed at an enemy with equal accuracy.

It was during the British occupation of Augusta, from 1778 to 1781, that Nancy became even more active, capturing Tories as well as scouting for the Americans. She ranged far and wide—from Augusta where she played the part of a madman to gain information about the British, throughout northeastern Georgia and even into South Carolina. Yet it was in her own one-room cabin on War Woman's Creek that Nancy Hart performed the feat for which she is best remembered.

Nancy was working in her cabin one day when the sound of hoofbeats brought her racing into the yard. A galloping horse usually meant trouble in those desperate days of British occupation, and this time was no exception.

As soon as she recognized the approaching rider as one of the "Liberty Boys," she knew the Tories must be in hot pursuit. So signaling the fleeing fugitive to turn into her yard, she ran ahead to open the front and back doors of the cabin. The rider then galloped through the cabin to hide in the swamp out back.

Nancy reclosed both doors without a minute to spare. The pursuing Tories were then pulling their horses to a stop at the front gate. When they questioned her, Nancy vowed that absolutely no one had come past her house—which really was the truth, since the rider had gone *through* it.

The Tories did not believe her, so she added, as if with great reluctance, "But I did see someone turn off into the woods a few hundred yards down the road."

This time the Tories thought she was telling the truth, and went flying down the road on a wild-goose chase. The chuckling Nancy then returned to her cabin, satisfied that she had saved at least one Liberty Boy from hanging.

The matter was far from settled, however. When the Tories realized that Nancy must have tricked them, they vowed revenge. And a few days later, a party set out from Augusta.

Rampaging across the countryside, they savagely murdered an American militia officer named Colonel Dooley. Then six of them separated from the main group and headed for the lone cabin on War Woman's Creek.

Except for one of her daughters, Nancy was alone when they rode up. Still she faced them boldly as they demanded to know whether she had lied about the Liberty Boy who had escaped their noose.

"Of course I did!" she stated defiantly.

It was the one answer the Tories hadn't expected, and for a few moments they stood there in surprised silence. Then one of them demanded that Nancy feed them while they decided what to do with her.

The dauntless Nancy replied that previous Tory raids

had left her without even a cow or a chicken, so she had no food to give them.

Spotting an old turkey in the corner of the yard, the enraged Tory leader lifted his gun and shot the bird. "Now cook it for us!" he growled as he handed it to her.

While she was preparing the turkey, Nancy sent her daughter Sukey to the spring for water. Unable to talk with the girl in front of the six Tories, she could only hope Sukey would remember the conch shell hidden in a tree stump in the swamp. The shell had been put there for just such an emergency. A few breaths blown into it would summon Benjamin Hart, who was working with some other farmers just beyond the swamp.

Meanwhile, Nancy made sure the Tories had all they wanted of her homemade wine. As they relaxed around the table, joking about what they were going to do with her, Nancy eyed the muskets they had stacked against the cabin wall.

Pretending to be busy with her cooking, she managed to pull out several wedges of pine wood which were used as chinking between the logs of the cabin wall. Then, as the Tories waxed merrier over their drinks, she quietly slipped one gun after the other through the hole between the logs.

Only two guns were left when one of the Tories discovered what she was doing. He lunged toward her—

but not fast enough. The musket in Nancy's hand spoke first.

Since each musket held only a single charge, Nancy tossed the gun aside and grabbed the remaining one, which she leveled at the other Tories.

"She can't get all of us with one shot!" the leader shouted. "Let's rush her!"

Without hesitation, Nancy pulled the trigger of the last musket, downing the Tory leader and temporarily halting the others.

That was all the time she needed, for just as the four Tories were about to charge, Nancy's daughter rushed in with one of the loaded muskets she had found outside.

"Father is on his way," Sukey reported, as she handed the loaded gun to her mother.

A few minutes later, Benjamin Hart arrived with the other men, who shouted that the Tories should be shot on the spot.

"They deserve what they gave Colonel Dooley," Nancy said bitterly. "But I think shooting is too good for them."

As a lieutenant in the Georgia militia, Benjamin Hart knew the decision was up to him. So without further discussion, he ordered that the Tories be taken out and hanged.

Because the British were still in command of that part of Georgia, the deaths of the six Tories were kept secret.

So it was not until many years after the war—and long after Nancy had moved on to Kentucky, where she died—that the story finally came out.

When it did, some historians voiced doubts that it had ever happened. And since there was no one still alive who had witnessed the event, there seemed no way to prove it had occurred.

Oddly enough, it was the six Tories who finally proved it—at least their skeletons did. When a railroad line was being constructed in the vicinity of the old Hart cabin, workmen uncovered an unmarked grave. Inside were the remains of the six Tories who had challenged the Amazon of War Woman's Creek.

WHAT CAN BE SEEN TODAY

GEORGIA: Perhaps the most fitting tribute to the "Amazon of War Woman's Creek" is the one described on an historical marker in La Grange, Georgia, which tells of a company of women soldiers formed during the Civil War to protect the town. They were called the Nancy Harts.

Hart County and the town of Hartwell in northern Georgia were named for her, as well as the highway (Route 77) leading from Elberton to Hartwell. Within the latter town, at the intersection of Carter and Benson streets, there is a granite marker commemorating her. Another monument is about a mile east of Hartwell, at the intersection of Routes 8 and 29.

A replica of Nancy Hart's cabin (with chimney stones from the original) can be seen in Nancy Hart State Park. Located off Route 17, about twelve miles south of Elberton, the park is open daily from spring through autumn.

Mary Hays

MONMOUTH'S MOLLY PITCHER

"Never has there been a day so hot!" the young woman panted when she reached the shaded spring.

While the bucket filled, she brushed her aching fingers against the lush grass of early summer. How she longed to sit in it if only for a few minutes—a few minutes away from the inferno-like heat of the battlefield.

Mary Hays did not sit down, however, for the heavy wooden bucket was now filled. And even though the cannonfire drowned out the cries of the men, her mind still heard their rasping voices begging for a pitcher of water. So hefting the bucket and trying to ignore the prickly rope handle that bit into her already raw palm, Mary started back.

The strength-sapping heat was even more intense as

she stumbled, half-crouching, across the field, sorely regretting the loss of the water that sloshed over the rim of the bucket.

"Watch out there!" she cried irritably, as a group of American soldiers rushed past her. "You'll spill the . . ."

Mary bit off her words abruptly when she realized the direction the soldiers were taking.

"You cowards!" she accused. "Get back to your guns!"

The soldiers ignored her, except for one burly Sergeant Major. "'Tis no desertion, Mistress," he said gruffly, his face a gray-black mask from the gunpowder that had been plastered on it by his own sweat. "General Lee has given the order for us to retreat."

"Retreat!" Mary echoed in disbelief. "Has Lee gone mad with the heat? Why, we're here to cut off the British retreat—not make one of our own! If we can stop them before they reach their fleet anchored off Sandy Hook . . ."

Again, Mary did not finish her sentence, for the Sergeant Major and his men had already moved on.

This time unmindful of the prostrating heat or of the water spilling out of the bucket, Mary raced across the field to where her husband John was manning one of the cannons. Before she reached him, however, the tall Pennsylvanian suddenly spun away from the cannon, clutching at a gaping wound.

Mary was soon at his side, staunching the blood with a shred of her white underskirt. She had just dipped her pitcher into the bucket, to give John a sip of water, when she heard a shouted order, "Abandon the cannon!"

Snatching up the gun swab that had fallen from her husband's hand, Mary cried out, "Stand fast, men! This gun must be kept blazing!"

History has not recorded how many—if any—of the gun crew remained with Mary Hays as she continued to load and fire the cannon. But it was George Washington himself who spotted the skirted figure as he rode out on the field—at least one gunner had not heeded General Lee's foolish order! Then within minutes, the enraged Washington halted the needless retreat.

General Nathanael Greene had also witnessed the heroism of the woman his soldiers called "Molly Pitcher," because of her untiring efforts to bring water to them. And after the battle Greene sought out Mary to thank her personally.

The next day, Greene went looking for her again. This time it was to bring her to General Washington, who had remembered the heroic woman standing fast while others ran. Greene found her still on the battlefield, helping to bring the wounded to a temporary hospital set up at the Tennent Church.

Mary, who had not rested since the battle, was presented to George Washington in the same ragged and powder-stained dress she had worn while firing the cannon. But if the General noticed, he did not indicate it, for he was about to do something he had never done before.

After thanking Mary Hays for her outstanding service, the Commander-in-Chief then commissioned her a sergeant in the Continental Army. It was a commission thoroughly approved of by all who had witnessed her daring act of the preceding day, or had their thirst relieved by "Molly's pitcher."

The story of "Sergeant Molly" soon spread throughout the army, and wherever she went she was cheered by the troops. She was even asked to review one regiment and, as she passed down the long line of soldiers, each one contributed a coin for a purse that was presented to her.

Mary's greatest reward, however, was the recovery of her husband John, whose place she had taken during the Battle of Monmouth. When the war was over, they returned to Carlisle, Pennsylvania, where they resumed their daily lives.

In time, little attention was given to the fact that Mary was indeed the famous "Molly Pitcher," and she worked as a charwoman while she raised her only son, also named John.

Yet the heroine of Monmouth, New Jersey, was not

destined to fade into obscurity. On February 21, 1822, when old age was weakening her once-strong body, she was awarded a pension by the state of Pennsylvania for her outstanding service during the Revolutionary War.

Ten years later, when she died at the age of seventy-eight, "Molly Pitcher" was buried with full military honors—as was befitting a sergeant of the Continental Army who had been personally commissioned by George Washington.

WHAT CAN BE SEEN TODAY

NEW JERSEY: On the green opposite the county courthouse in Freehold stands a tall shaft commemorating the Battle of Monmouth. One of its five bronze bas-reliefs depicts Mary Hays manning the cannon. At the western edge of the green is the Monmouth County Historical Association (70 Court Street—open daily except Monday and the last two weeks in July and December). On display at the museum there is a painting of her meeting with George Washington, as well as other articles pertaining to the Battle of Monmouth.

Approximately a mile to the northwest, the site of the battle-field includes the area on either side of the Englishtown Road (Route 522). At the railroad overpass, a dirt road to the north leads to the spring (now covered by an abandoned well house and marked by a plaque) where it is thought that Mary Hays drew water for the thirsting soldiers.

Unfortunately, the undeveloped Monmouth Battlefield State Park (on the left side of Route 522 near the boulder marked by a plaque commemorating the site where Washington met with General Lee) is still closed to the public. However, adjacent to this is the Cobb House (open daily) which serves as headquarters for the Battleground Historical Society and where maps of the battlefield are available.

A short distance to the west (via Route 522, then north on Monmouth County Road 3) is the Old Tennent Church (open 10 to 7). Many of the soldiers who died during the battle are buried in the cemetery there, and the church still contains a blood-stained pew on which a wounded soldier lay when Old Tennent was used as a field hospital.

PENNSYLVANIA: "Molly Pitcher" is buried in the Old Graveyard on South Street in Carlisle, where there are two monuments honoring her. The Cumberland County Historical Society Museum (21 North Pitt Street, Carlisle) has a pitcher belonging to the heroine, but it is not the one she used during the Battle of Monmouth.

Sally Townsend

FOR LOVE OF COUNTRY

The brush of satin over numerous petticoats was no more than a whisper in the silent room, yet Samuel Townsend heard it. Without looking up from his ledger, he gestured for his daughter Sally to sit next to him.

"You wished to see me?" she asked.

"Yes, Sarah."

The gay smile fled from the girl's lips. Whenever her father called her Sarah instead of Sally, it was a serious occasion.

"Let me have it," Townsend said suddenly. Then when he saw the look of bewilderment on her face, he added, "The valentine, Sarah. Colonel Simcoe's valentine to you."

"But . . . but how did you . . ." Sally faltered.

"The whole house is tittering over it," Townsend replied gruffly. "By tomorrow all of Oyster Bay will know of it. In fact, I'll be surprised if your brother Robert does not hear of it in New York. Now let me see it!"

Without another word, the dark-haired girl produced the valentine from a fold in her cashmere shawl. It did not go unnoticed by Samuel Townsend how gently she handled it, as if it were a treasured possession.

Quickly he read the flowery words, then repeated some of them in a disapproving rumble:

> To you my heart I must resign
> O choose me for your Valentine!
>
> "Fond youth," the God of Love replies,
> "Your answer take from Sarah's eyes."

When he was finished, the unsmiling man gazed at his lovely daughter for a few moments. "It seems our British boarder is quite smitten by you," Townsend finally said. "Nor do I have any quarrel with that." Again he paused. "Just as long as *you* are not smitten by *him!*"

The flush that burned Sally's face proved what her father had suspected.

"Under any other circumstances," he continued, "Colonel John Graves Simcoe would be an admirable choice as a husband."

The sympathy which had tinged his tone abruptly

vanished with his next words, "But Simcoe is now the enemy!"

Sally shuddered, but did not answer.

"Daughter, do you forget how the British arrested me when they took over Long Island? Do you ignore the fact that they have also taken over our home? Do you realize what would happen if they found out about the messages we send to Robert?"

Trembling, Sally Townsend arose from her chair. "I understand, Father," she said as she reached for the ornate valentine. "You need not worry about me."

Samuel Townsend did worry, however. For as the months passed and Colonel Simcoe continued to live at Raynham Hall, it was impossible to keep Sally away from the dashing officer of the Queens Rangers. Nor was it practical to do so.

As a known patriot, Townsend's freedom was always in jeopardy. Only by keeping his unwelcome guests content could he escape the horror of a British prison ship—and that contentment was due in part to the charming company of his three daughters, Audrey, Phebe, and Sally.

There was another reason, too. While the British were quartered in his house, there was always the possibility that Samuel Townsend might find out some vital information that could be passed on to General Washington.

When such an opportunity came, however, it was Sally Townsend who uncovered the secret. Then she was forced to choose between the man she loved and the newborn country struggling to survive.

Strangely enough, a simple cupboard and a plate of doughnuts would be responsible for the historic events about to unfold.

For several months, British Major John André had been coming to Raynham Hall to visit his friend Colonel Simcoe. When there, he often took part in the gay parties the sisters held, sometimes playing boyish pranks like hiding a plate of doughnuts that Sally had just fried.

This practical joke was brought to mind one day when Sally was alone in the kitchen, preparing the same type of doughnuts. Busy at work in one corner, she was startled to see a man stealthily come in through the back door. Though he looked around, he did not see Sally who, stunned into silence, remained in her corner.

As she watched in amazement, the man deposited a letter in the cupboard, then quickly left the kitchen.

Waiting a few minutes to make certain the man didn't return, Sally then rushed over to the cupboard. Examination revealed only what appeared to be a routine business letter addressed to someone called John Anderson.

But who was John Anderson? And why had the man hidden the letter in the Townsend kitchen cupboard?

Perhaps it was only a joke, but Sally decided she would watch to see who came to retrieve the message.

Before long, Major John André entered the kitchen. Not seeing anyone, he headed directly for the cupboard, and took out the letter. Then picking up the plate of doughnuts, Major André hid them in the cupboard, just as he had done before. Obviously it was an excuse for his presence in the kitchen, should he be detected. But Sally made no move and he left without seeing her in the corner.

Intuition as much as curiosity made Sally pause later in the day when she heard Major André's voice coming from behind the closed door of Colonel Simcoe's room. The conversation was muted, but her keen ears still picked up a few of the words: "West Point . . . John Anderson . . . West Point . . . West Point . . ."

The repeated reference to the still unfinished fortress fifty miles to the northwest on the Hudson River sent a shiver through Sally's slim frame. How often she had heard her father and brother mention the importance of West Point. If the British captured West Point, they would control the Hudson River!

Sally waited no longer. Whatever they were discussing about West Point must be vitally important—something the Americans should know about.

At that time, Sally Townsend had no idea of the extent of her brother Robert's activities as a spy for

George Washington. All she knew was that he was presently in New York City, working as a merchant and journalist, and that he had asked his family to send him any interesting information they might overhear about the British. (Actually, Robert Townsend was one of Washington's best secret agents, who worked under the code name of Culper Jr.)

Pretending she needed a certain type of tea that was available only in her brother's New York store, Sally managed to send a message by one of the market boats going down Long Island Sound.

That was how Robert Townsend received the news which led to the discovery of a secret plot to betray West Point to the British. For Major André (otherwise known as John Anderson) was then negotiating with General Benedict Arnold, the most infamous traitor in American history.

The plot was later foiled by André's capture behind the American lines in September, 1780, and he was executed shortly thereafter. As for the traitor, Arnold, he escaped aboard the British brig-of-war *Vulture*—but without the plans the Redcoats had wanted. West Point was safe!

Meanwhile, the long years of war went on for the inhabitants of Raynham Hall. Despite her personal feelings, Sally knew the futility of any relationship with Colonel Simcoe. And when he finally went away from

Oyster Bay, later to become Lieutenant Governor of Upper Canada, there were no tears in Sally's eyes—at least not in public.

She never discussed her relationship with the colonel, and most people presumed it had been only a flirtation— a flirtation prompted by her desire to keep her father from being arrested again, and to obtain information as to the movements of the British.

And so it was that Sally Townsend's secret was kept hidden until her death in 1842. At that time, a faded valentine—dog-eared from many readings—was found among her possessions. It was this memento, plus the fact that Sally had never married, which finally indicated the full story of this heroic girl who had put love of country before her own happiness.

WHAT CAN BE SEEN TODAY

NEW YORK: The home of the Townsend family, Raynham Hall, is located on West Main Street in the town of Oyster Bay on Long Island (open daily except Tuesday). Among the many historic items pertaining to the time the British officers were quartered there is the cupboard where Major André hid the plate of doughnuts, as well as a pane of glass etched to "the adorable Miss Sally [Sarah] Townsend." She is buried in the Townsend Cemetery, on the south side of Fort Hill, Oyster Bay.

Hannah Hendee

"GIVE ME MY SON!"

The single shriek shredded the early morning quiet. Then as if that first scream had loosed all the others in the world, the small Vermont village erupted in ear-shattering sound. The high-pitched yelps of the attacking Indians were counterpointed by the rumbling shouts of the British officers who led them. Keening women searched for wailing children, while hoarse-voiced men ran to aid their families.

Then a more ominous sound was heard—the whoosh and crackle of wind-driven flames devouring one of the thirty-seven buildings that would be burned that day.

Because she lived some distance from the initial attack, Hannah Hendee heard none of these things. For her, the first sound of danger came with the frantic pounding on the door by her boarder, Mr. Chafee.

"Indian raid!" he shouted. "They've burned Royalton! And now they're heading this way!"

As Hannah quickly dressed her two children, her husband Robert told her to bring them to a neighbor's house, while he went on to warn the people of Bethel.

Taking her daughter Lucretia in her arms and seven-year-old Michael by the hand, Hannah set off through the woods. Before she had gone very far, however, a group of Indians came running toward her. Jerking Michael from her grasp, they set off again without touching either Hannah or her baby daughter.

The terrified woman screamed, "Give me back my son! Where are you taking him?"

Fortunately, the Indians were of the Caghnewaga tribe from Canada and spoke some English. One of them halted long enough to say that Michael would make a good Indian warrior. Then he disappeared down the forest trail, dragging the screaming boy along with him.

The fact that the Indians had not harmed her gave Hannah the courage to follow after the renegade band. All she knew was that somehow—someway—she must get Michael away from them. But the Indians were much faster and by the time she came to the bank of the White River, Hannah had lost sight of them.

What she did see now was the destruction—all of the houses and barns dotting the valley were burning, the flames more brilliant than the autumn foliage. In the distance, scattered groups of people were milling around aimlessly . . . homelessly . . . helplessly.

Then Hannah spotted several Tories with a party of Indians. In their arms were various articles looted from the now burning homes, while they drove before them three young boys.

"Where are you taking the children? What are you going to do with them?" Hannah demanded, unmindful of the danger she was in.

"Why, the Indians will kill them, that's what!" one of the Tories jeered. Then he laughed as Hannah gasped.

But the war party was not interested in this lone woman carrying a child. Intent on their mission of destruction, they continued on past her, as she turned once more toward the river.

"I must find Michael," she kept repeating. "I must save him!"

Slowly a plan was forming in her mind. The presence of the Tories showed that the Indians had not planned this devastating raid alone. If there were Tories, then there had to be a leader somewhere. If she could find that man . . .

Across the river she could see a large number of Indians. Perhaps that was their rallying point—the place the commander would be.

She was just about to ford the fast-moving river when an Indian came up to her. This one, she soon found, did not speak English, but it was obvious he thought she was surrendering. So by using sign language, he told her he would carry her daughter across.

Having gained the opposite bank, Hannah soon found the British officer who had accompanied the Indians from Canada. Lieutenant Horton greeted her politely, as if they were meeting at some tea party instead of the chill Vermont woods. Then he went on to assure her he had given orders that women and children were not to be harmed. As for the boys taken prisoner, they would not be killed either. They would be trained as Indian warriors.

"No child will be able to endure the long trek back to Canada!" Hannah cried. "They will die before you reach there! Have you no mercy? Have the British become such savages that they murder children?"

Suddenly fearful that her bold words might infuriate the British officer, Hannah then implored, "Give me my son! Don't let him die!"

The officer shook his head. "These Indians do not give up what they take."

"You are their leader," Hannah persisted. "And they must obey you. Order them to give me my son!"

For long moments Lieutenant Horton studied the distraught but still lovely face of the woman before him. Then he stood up suddenly. "As soon as the group arrives, you shall have your son."

A short time later, Michael Hendee was dragged into the clearing by his captors. Hannah waited breathlessly while Lieutenant Horton spoke with the Indian holding her son's hand. Harsh words were exchanged, but finally the boy was delivered to her.

"But you must stay here awhile," Lieutenant Horton told Hannah. "There are still scouting parties out, and they might take your son from you again. As soon as they return, you may leave for home."

The grateful Hannah sought to thank him, but Lieutenant Horton merely walked away to greet a newly arrived band of Indians and Tories. With them were some other children who had been captured. As soon as the boys saw Hannah, they raced over to her, their faces tear-streaked and frightened, begging her to help them.

Meanwhile, an old Indian came over to where Michael sat next to his mother and sister. Without a word, he swooped down to grab Michael's hand. But Hannah was just as quick, and held onto her son as the Indian tried to pull him away. Only when the Indian began swinging a cutlass did Hannah release her hold, fearing that Michael would be struck.

Just then, Lieutenant Horton strode up. After a few minutes of heated debate with the Indian, Horton re-

turned Michael to Hannah, telling her, "You can start back to Royalton now."

"But how can I leave those other poor children behind?" Hannah asked. "Some of them are younger than my Michael. They will surely die if you attempt to march them all the way to Canada!"

To her amazement, the British officer nodded. "You may take the others with you too—and Godspeed."

Not daring to wait a second longer, Hannah lifted her daughter into her arms. Then with eight other boys following behind Michael, they set out on the long journey home.

There was still a river to cross, but the danger of its rapidly flowing water did not frighten Hannah after what she had been through. The two smallest children she carried on her back, while the others formed a human chain and they carefully waded across.

It was late in the day and Hannah knew they would never reach Royalton before dark. So after walking the children another three miles to warm their river-chilled bodies, she clustered them around her and they spent a shivering night in the woods.

The next morning the people of Royalton were going about the sad business of sifting through the cinders of their burned-out homes, when someone spotted the line of straggling figures on the crest of a hill.

Exuberant shouts filled the air and even those who

had lost loved ones in the raid felt a surge of gladness as Hannah Hendee brought home the children she had so daringly saved.

WHAT CAN BE SEEN TODAY

VERMONT: On the eastern side of the Green in South Royalton is a memorial arch honoring Hannah Hendee (spelled "Handy" on the arch). There are also two markers pertaining to the 1780 raid, one of which mentions Mrs. Hendee, on the common in Royalton Village on Route 14.

———◄◆►———

Tempe Wick

MUTINY AT JOCKEY HOLLOW

Tempe's name was really Temperance, but it should have been Temper, considering the way she felt right now.

Here it was, the first day of the new year 1781, and already she had ridden clear to Mendham. It was bitterly cold—almost as cold as last winter when all those soldiers had died over in Jockey Hollow.

Tempe shivered when she remembered that, and the shiver seemed to chase away her anger. After all, she was young and healthy—not dead like her father and those poor soldiers, or sick like her mother. And it had not been difficult to ride the few miles to Mendham to tell her brother-in-law, Dr. William Leddell, that her mother wanted to see him.

No, the ride through the New Jersey countryside

wasn't what had made Tempe angry. It was that bunch of soldiers up ahead, waving for her to stop. What did they want, anyway? She was cold and she needed to get home.

Tempe was almost up to them, when instinct made her jerk back on the reins in a vain attempt to wheel her horse around. Just as she did, a figure darted toward her. In one quick lunge, the horse's bridle was being clutched firmly, preventing any escape.

Fear swept over Tempe as she stared down into the wildly bearded face of the man holding the bridle.

"Wh . . . what do you want?" she managed to gasp.

"Easy, lass. We're not out to hurt you. We're not the British."

"I can see that!" Tempe blurted out. Then she was immediately sorry when the bearded soldier glanced shamefully down at his tattered uniform.

By now the ragtag band had surrounded her, making Tempe's fear-filled heart thud painfully.

"Who are you? What do you want?" she repeated, hoping her voice wouldn't quiver and that the soldiers wouldn't see her trembling hands.

"We're men of the Pennsylvania Line," a tall sergeant answered. "And what we want is your horse."

"My horse! Why, it's the only one we have left!" Tempe told him. "Did General Wayne order you to . . ."

"Get on with it, Sergeant," a voice interrupted. "And then let's be on our way to Philadelphia."

Tempe stared down at the sergeant, whose bare toes were protruding from his broken boots. "He . . . he said Philadelphia. But you told me you were part of the Pennsylvania Line. Why, they're camped over in Jockey Hollow. General Washington means for them to defend New Jersey if the British attack."

Breathless from her outburst, Tempe stopped abruptly when the sergeant nodded.

"Aye, we'll defend New Jersey," he said. "But first we're going to Philadelphia to see the Congress. We've not been paid for twelve months now. Few of us have blankets and none of us have enough clothing in this accursed cold . . ."

"Our enlistments are up too," said a man next to the sergeant.

"And we haven't been paid a single paper dollar! Those new recruits, though, they even get a bonus!" This last bitter remark came from a figure huddled under a tree, his bandaged feet drawn up to a small fire which Tempe hadn't noticed before.

"So, we're heading for Philadelphia," the sergeant concluded.

"But that . . . that's desertion!" Tempe exclaimed.

"No, Miss." The sergeant shook his head slowly. "We're just going to Philadelphia to demand our rights from the Continental Congress. No one can expect us to stay here and freeze to death."

With a shudder, Tempe realized the truth of his words. Only last winter more than a hundred soldiers of the First Connecticut Brigade had died over in Jockey Hollow. The British had not killed them—with little food and even less shelter, sickness and exposure had been more deadly than any cannonball.

"And you want my horse?" Tempe barely whispered.

"Not me, Miss," the sergeant answered. "Him and another." He was pointing to the soldier with the bandaged feet. "Frostbit his feet are. He can't walk and we can't leave him here."

Sympathy washed over Tempe. Then it quickly ebbed as she remembered her own sick mother, who lay waiting for her in the lonely farmhouse down the road. Without a horse, they would be stranded there, two women alone . . . Surely the soldiers could carry the sick men to the army hospital nearby. As for their planned mutiny, no matter what their reason, it was still mutiny —and they would leave New Jersey undefended.

Suddenly Tempe knew what she must do.

Forcing her lips to smile, she nodded her head and bent forward in the saddle, her arms extended to the blue-eyed sergeant. Just as she expected, his hands immediately released the bridle in order to help her to dismount.

"Giddap!" Tempe shouted, grabbing the reins. At the same time she gave the horse a powerful kick with her booted heels.

The small band of soldiers scattered before the charging horse, and in a few minutes Tempe had left them far behind.

Never allowing the tired horse to slow his pace, Tempe raced for home. Down the frozen dirt road, past the winter-withered fields and orchard, straight through the herb garden, pulling to a stop only long enough to unlatch the farmhouse door.

In the few minutes it had taken her to gallop the mile home, she had realized the futility of putting the horse in the barn. The sergeant and his men would surely follow her, and she and her mother would be powerless against them. As for hiding the horse in the woods, even if the sergeant didn't follow the tracks, the now overheated and tired animal would perish from the intense cold.

There was only one other way, she decided, hoping that her shocking plan wouldn't make her mother any sicker than she already was.

Sliding off the horse's back, Tempe quickly led him through the kitchen of the farmhouse, then into her mother's bedroom. She heard her mother's gasp from the bed, and paused only long enough to tell the sick woman why she was doing such an odd thing. Then

Tempe brought the animal into her own small bedroom. There she remained, holding the head of the horse so he wouldn't snort or whinny, as she waited for the soldiers she knew would come.

They came all right, within the hour. And for an hour they searched the barn and the surrounding woods. Fortunately, the snow had been trampled so much in the yard in front of the house that there were no clear-cut tracks leading to the door. So not once did the soldiers think of looking inside the house. After all, who would bring a horse inside a house? No one but Tempe Wick —a young farm girl who, though she sympathized with the soldiers' plight, refused to help them in their mutiny.

Tempe Wick's action that New Year's Day may have contributed in part to the successful resolution of the mutiny. For had some of the soldiers not been delayed by her, the whole body of mutineers might not have met their commander, Major General Anthony Wayne, later that night.

When Wayne called for them to turn back, they refused to do so. However, they promised they would if the British tried to attack. As further proof of their loyalty, they turned over to Wayne two British agents who had learned of the mutiny and had tried to convince the Pennsylvanians to come over to the British side.

When the Continental Congress heard of this, they agreed that the men of the Pennsylvania Line were really loyal soldiers with a just grievance who had been driven to desperate means. And by January 7, 1781—

only six days after the ragged band had confronted Tempe—the soldiers' complaints had been settled. In fact, many of the Pennsylvanians who were due to be discharged from the army later re-enlisted to continue the defense of New Jersey.

WHAT CAN BE SEEN TODAY

NEW JERSEY: The New Jersey farmhouse where Tempe Wick hid her horse is now part of Morristown National Historical Park, and is located on the north side of Tempe Wick Road, a few hundred feet west of Jockey Hollow Road. It is open to visitors every afternoon except Thanksgiving, February through November.

Approximately five miles away from Morristown, New Jersey, is the Ford Mansion (on Morris Street near Ridgedale Avenue). Behind the mansion, which at one time served as George Washington's headquarters, is a museum where Tempe Wick's red cape is on display, as well as other articles pertaining to the encampment at Jockey Hollow. Both museum and mansion are open every day except Thanksgiving, Christmas, and New Year's Day.

Elizabeth Champe

IN DEFENSE OF A TRAITOR

Sergeant Major John Champe did not have to ask his wife if she had heard the news about him. He could see the answer in her eyes as she stood there, one hand raised to her suddenly chalk-white face.

Of course, she had been shocked by his unexpected arrival at their home in Loudoun County, Virginia. But was that the only reason she continued to stand there in the doorway staring at him? Or was it because she believed he . . .

At that moment, Elizabeth Champe found her voice. "Oh, my poor husband!" she cried, as she ran to him. "I don't know why they are saying such things about you—why they are hunting for you. I only know that whatever happened, you are not a traitor!"

That simple declaration of love and faith gave the

exhausted man new strength, and he followed his wife inside the house he had left so many months ago. First, he must be shown the new baby born during his absence. Then he must tell Elizabeth everything that had happened. And finally, after she understood why he had been branded a traitor, he must say good-bye.

Had Elizabeth been aware of this last part, she might not have sat there so quietly. As it was, she said not a word while John told her what had happened to him since that fateful day in September, 1780.

His company had been camped in New Jersey when the shocking news came that the commander of West Point, General Benedict Arnold, had committed treason. Even more galling was the fact that Arnold had escaped down the Hudson River to the British in New York City.

The infuriated George Washington wanted Arnold brought back to stand trial, and even had negotiated with the British to trade the captured Major John André (Arnold's British contact) for the traitor. When these negotiations fell through, Washington had been left with only one choice: send a secret agent to New York to kidnap Arnold!

Sergeant Major John Champe was selected for this mission.

Following a plan known only to Washington and Colonel "Lighthorse Harry" Lee, on October 19, 1780,

Champe had pretended to desert his company and offer his services to the British in New York City. Since he also carried along his company's daybook, which contained vital information concerning American activities, the British believed his story. He was then assigned to the newly formed Loyalist Legion commanded by the turncoat Benedict Arnold.

It was a perfect setup for Champe, and within a few weeks he had completed arrangements for the abduction of Arnold. However, on the very day Arnold was to be kidnapped, the Loyalist Legion was ordered to Virginia. His plan destroyed, there was nothing Champe could do but go along, hoping for another opportunity.

By the time the British troop ship anchored in the James River on January 4, 1781, Champe had realized something that would drastically alter his plans. As a member of the Loyalist Legion, he would be expected to fight his fellow Americans—and on his own native soil of Virginia. This he would not—could not—do. And as soon as he could, John Champe deserted Arnold's Loyalist Legion.

Hunted now by both the British and Americans, Champe eventually reached General Washington, who was then headquartered in Williamsburg, Virginia. And it was there John Champe received the worst disappointment of his life.

Rather than publicly exonerating the sergeant and

returning him to his company, George Washington decided it would be safer for Champe if he went into hiding for awhile. The general then gave Champe an honorable discharge, and offered him some land in the Shenandoah Mountains. This Champe refused, saying he already owned a tract of wilderness land farther to the west.

"So that is where I must go," Champe concluded his story to his wife.

"You mean that is where *we* must go," Elizabeth quietly corrected him.

The tired man slowly shook his head. "The land I own on Abraham's Creek is utter wilderness, with not even a cabin for you and the children. I cannot ask you to go there, Elizabeth."

"You did not ask me, John," she pointed out. "As for a cabin, I suppose we will just have to build one!"

And so it was that a short time later John and Elizabeth Champe set out for the wilderness of what is now West Virginia. Accompanying them and their four children was one of George Washington's most trusted servants, a man named Sam. Washington had told Sam to stay with the Champes until they were settled, then return to Mount Vernon.

The first leg of the journey took them to the home of a close friend, Colonel Joseph Neville, near Moorehead in a valley of the Alleghenies. There Elizabeth and the children stayed for a week until John had located their tract of land on Abraham's Creek.

The change from her comfortable home in Loudoun County to a primitive cabin in the wilderness must have been extremely difficult for Elizabeth. But she hid her fears and loneliness behind a cheerful smile, hoping by her own example to keep her husband from brooding.

As it was, John often took solitary walks through the surrounding woodlands. Just as often, Elizabeth would go looking for him, to sit with him awhile and point out the beauties of their wilderness home. She even began to call their rude cabin by the fanciful name of Ornicello, in recognition of the many birds whose songs brightened the dark days of their exile.

From time to time, a visitor sent by Washington would bring news of the war's progress. Occasionally, too, there came terse warnings that Champe was still being hunted. Then finally one day two years later, Washington's servant Sam arrived with a message that the war was over and it would be safe for them to return to Loudoun County.

Only then did Elizabeth reveal how much she had missed her former home. She did not weep with joy as many women might have done. Instead, she had her family—now numbering six children—ready to leave as soon as John said the word.

The time Elizabeth did weep was when they reached

Loudoun County to find that Martha Washington had traveled forty miles from Mount Vernon to make the house ready for their arrival.

It was a fitting reward for Elizabeth Champe, whose loyalty and courage had sustained her husband through the long years of exile. Yet it was a reward she had little time to enjoy.

Soon enough, a worried George Washington visited them. Perhaps, he said, he had been hasty in telling them to return. The peace declaration had done little to end the violence and bitterness on both sides, and many a man was bent on revenge. What if one of them recognized John Champe?

Washington's meaning was only too apparent. They were not safe in Loudoun County, after all.

Once more, Elizabeth Champe packed their belongings and they headed west, first to Ornicello and later to Kentucky. Ever was she by the side of the man who had given up so much for so little—ever did she hope that someday her husband would be recognized for the selfless patriot he was.

Unfortunately, neither Elizabeth nor John lived to enjoy that recognition. For it was not until 1847 that the United States Congress voted Champe a posthumous promotion, declaring that his had been "one of the most courageous acts of the American Revolution."

No less could be said for his loyal wife Elizabeth.

WHAT CAN BE SEEN TODAY

WEST VIRGINIA: On Route 28, north of Mouth of Seneca, West Virginia, there is a highway marker pointing out two giant formations called Champe Rocks, named in honor of the Revolutionary hero.

Deborah Sampson

ALIAS ROBERT SHURTLEFF

"Spinster!" Deborah Sampson muttered, as she angrily pushed the needle through the unyielding fustian cloth.

"So what if I'm twenty-one and unmarried? Is being a spinster any worse than marrying that dolt Mother has chosen for me?"

Over and over the needle flashed in the late afternoon sunshine. Then, when the last button was sewn on, Deborah held the man's jacket against her own shoulders.

"No, marriage is not for me!" she declared to her image in the mirror. "There's too much to be seen beyond these Massachusetts hills—even if I must do so as a man!"

Late that night, Deborah slipped away from her house, wearing the man's suit she had secretly made. It was more than seventy miles from Middleboro to Worcester, Massachusetts, but the determined young woman walked the full distance. There, on May 23, 1782, she was mustered into the army under the name of Robert Shurtleff.

Surprising as it may be that she managed to fool the muster master when she enlisted, it is even more amazing how she kept up her deception for more than a year. Needless to say, she had many close calls, the first one coming only a few weeks after her enlistment when her company was sent to West Point.

Since Deborah had left home without telling anyone, her family—as well as the "dolt" her mother had been pressuring her to marry—had been searching for her. It was the young suitor who, while looking for her in New York State, chanced to visit West Point. The horrified Deborah spotted him, but he did not recognize her among the other uniformed men she was marching with at the time.

The experience made Deborah realize that, no matter what her differences were with her mother, it was not right to worry her family. So she sent off a letter, saying merely that they were not to be "too much troubled," for she was all right and had joined "a large but well-regulated family."

With her conscience thus cleared, Deborah then concentrated on soldiering—and avoiding detection. She was

soon to find out that the former was much more easily accomplished than the latter.

From a physical standpoint, she had bound her chest with a heavy bandage to diminish her ample curves. As for her beardless face, many a young soldier had no need of a razor. And to explain her deftness with a needle, she told her barracks mates that she was an only son who had been forced to help with household duties.

The other soldiers often kidded about her good looks, calling her a "blooming boy." But this was only good-natured raillery, for the blonde, blue-eyed Deborah was well liked and looked upon as someone who never shirked a duty.

Muscles hardened by years of heavy farmwork helped her through that first long summer of 1782 when the oppressive heat and long marches caused many a new soldier to fall by the wayside. But farmwork had not prepared Deborah for the blood and terror of her first bayonet charge, and she later reported that was the only time she almost faltered.

Nor was she prepared for the general order that during the hot weather *all* soldiers must bathe in the river each day. Deborah solved that one, however, by taking a swim before the other soldiers woke up in the morning.

An even more ticklish situation developed when Deborah's company encountered a band of Tories near East

Chester (just north of New York City), and she was wounded in the thigh. Ever fearful of detection, she crawled off to probe for the musketball herself, and did not return to camp until she was no longer in need of medical attention.

As winter approached, Deborah's company was sent north to Ticonderoga, where they fought marauding Indians, and she proved herself an able soldier. Because of this, in 1783, General Paterson chose "Private Robert Shurtleff" as his orderly, and Deborah accompanied him to Philadelphia.

It was there that Deborah was faced with one of the most perplexing—and hilarious—experiences of her army career. A young woman fell in love with her! Embarrassed for herself as well as the amorous lady, Deborah had a difficult time convincing her admirer that romance was definitely out of the question.

This was the least of Deborah's problems, though, for it was also in Philadelphia that her true identity was discovered. An epidemic of "malignant fever" (probably what we call meningitis today) was raging through the Philadelphia encampment, and the hard-working Deborah soon fell victim to it.

As she lay near death in an army hospital, a doctor checking for her heartbeat discovered the bandage wrapped tightly around her chest—and then the reason why.

Shortly after she recovered, Deborah was brought before General John Paterson, fully expecting a severe reprimand or even worse punishment. But startled though he was, the general felt he could not ignore her many months of loyal service. Whether man or woman, Private Robert Shurtleff deserved an honorable discharge. So that was what General Paterson awarded Deborah Sampson, the only woman in the Revolution known to have enlisted and served as a man.

The story of Deborah Sampson would not be complete without mentioning that she eventually abandoned her declaration that marriage was not for her. Those words had been meant for the "dolt" her mother had chosen for her, but not for Benjamin Gannett, whom she married soon after the war was over. Benjamin and Deborah then settled down in Sharon, Massachusetts, where they raised three children.

It was not the end of Deborah's public life, however. When her son and two daughters were grown, she began lecturing on her wartime experiences. Deborah became a great favorite in Boston and other northeastern cities, where she ended her talk with a well-executed Manual of Arms. Thus she became one of the first women lecturers to tour the United States—a fitting finale to her daring days of disguise.

WHAT CAN BE SEEN TODAY

MASSACHUSETTS: In the small town of Plympton, Massachusetts, where Deborah Sampson was born, there is a monument to her on Main Street, adjacent to the Soldiers' Memorial. Nearby, at 46 Elm Street, is the Deborah Sampson House (presently under private ownership).

Approximately thirty miles to the northwest, in Sharon, there is a monument marking her grave in Rock Ridge Cemetery. (The entrance is on Mountain Street; the monument is in the section of the cemetery bordering East Street.) At 300 East Street, about a mile from the cemetery, is the house (not open to the public) where Deborah Sampson spent her last years. Nearby is a street named in her honor.

Phebe Reynolds

A DEBT OF COURAGE

At first she thought it was a dream. For she still had nightmares about the time Claudius Smith's gang of cowboys had attacked her home. And in the few minutes it took her to wake up fully, eleven-year-old Phebe Reynolds once again relived that night of terror.

Three years ago, Claudius Smith had been hanged at Goshen, New York. But that had not stopped the Tory outlaw's band. It only made them more vicious. For then they swore revenge on all the patriots who had anything to do with the death of their leader. And Phebe's father, Henry Reynolds, had been one of those patriots.

The cowboys—called that because of their thefts of cattle—kept their word. On the night Phebe still dreamed about, they had tried to force their way into the Reynolds farmhouse. Though they found the doors had been securely locked and the heavy window shutters barred, the cowboys refused to give up. Instead, they had climbed on the roof, determined to slide down the wide chimney just like St. Nicholas—only the gifts they carried were bullets and blades.

As Phebe sat up in bed, she remembered it had been her mother who had thought of the featherbed that night. Quickly ripping open the ticking, Mrs. Reynolds had tossed the feathers on the fire. The resulting nostril-searing stench cloud rising up the chimney had successfully routed the outlaws. But they had sworn they would return to the isolated farmhouse.

Was this the night?

Phebe strained to hear the sound that had awakened her.

Hoofbeats—that's what it was. Someone riding into the farmyard. Again she listened. No, it was more than one. Maybe a half dozen horses out there in the dead of night. Was it . . .

"Open up!" a rough voice ordered. "We're a detachment of soldiers sent by General Washington to hunt down deserters!"

The young girl heaved a sigh of relief. "They're our men," she murmured happily. Then hearing her father descending the stairs to let in the patriot soldiers, she lay back down and pulled the covers over her.

She was almost asleep again when Henry Reynolds' pain-filled cry echoed through the house.

Pausing only to pull a dress over her nightgown, Phebe raced for the stairs. But even though far advanced in pregnancy, Phebe's mother was already ahead of the girl.

As they entered the kitchen, a blood-smeared Henry Reynolds was being dragged across the floor by a bearded man waving a sword.

"He . . . he's not a patriot!" Mrs. Reynolds cried. "He's Benjamin Kelley, the cowboy! And he's killed my Henry!"

"Not yet," Kelley snarled, as he continued to drag the unconscious man toward the fireplace. Then he turned to another of the outlaws. "Sling that rope over the trammel pole up there."

At these last words, Mrs. Reynolds moved toward the bearded outlaw. Then suddenly she clutched at her stomach as if in great pain, and fell unconscious to the floor.

Phebe was afraid her mother might be going into premature labor, but she could not help her now. For already the outlaws had placed a noose around her father's neck and were hoisting him up to hang from the trammel pole.

"Stop!" Phebe screamed, as she lunged at Benjamin Kelley.

Although Phebe was large and robust, she was no match for the outlaw, who flung her away with a back-handed blow that stunned her.

Strangled gasps were escaping from Henry Reynolds' purpled lips when Phebe regained her senses. The half dozen cowboys were tearing through the kitchen cupboards, so they did not see her snatch a knife from the bread board. With one quick movement, Phebe leaped on the hearthstone stool. Then a frantic slash severed the rope that held the feebly struggling man.

She had just loosened the noose around her father's neck when one of the cowboys turned around. "Get away, girl!" he shouted.

Phebe did not move.

"Away, I said," he raged, "or you'll get the same!"

By this time the others had joined him, knives and swords pointing at Phebe. Only then did she move—but not out of the way.

Spinning around, Phebe flung herself down on the crumpled form of Henry Reynolds, shielding his body with her own. Benjamin Kelley tried to lift her but she clung to her father and the outlaw could not separate them.

Picking up the rope which had fallen from the trammel pole, Kelley lashed out viciously. Phebe's body quivered at each blow of the rope, but she did not cry out. Nor did she release her hold.

It took four of the outlaws to pry her loose. The unconscious Henry Reynolds was then hanged once more from the trammel pole, after which the outlaws resumed their looting of the house. Certain they had snuffed out the life of Henry Reynolds, they did not prevent Phebe from cutting him down a second time.

They had not reckoned with the strength of the farmer, however. When they returned to the kitchen, they found Phebe bent over the still-breathing man. Seeing them enter, she once more shielded her father's body with her own.

This time, the outlaws lost all control. Knives and fists slashed and pounded the two helpless bodies until the cowboys' rage was replaced by exhaustion, and the oaken floor was slippery with blood.

After dumping the body of Henry Reynolds into a huge chest, they picked up the loot they had collected and set fire to several rooms. Then they rode away from the isolated farmhouse, confident that the fire would consume all evidence of their vengeful raid.

Miraculously—for that is the only word to describe it —none of the Reynolds family died that night. In fact, their number was increased by one, for Mrs. Reynolds gave birth to a premature but healthy baby girl not long after the outlaws left.

Although severely injured, the courageous Phebe had managed to smother the fires the cowboys had set and

to rescue Henry Reynolds from the chest. Though at first he seemed dead, Phebe battled to revive him, then began bandaging his many wounds.

Still the long July night was not over for eleven-year-old Phebe. The alarm must be sounded. The neighbors must be warned that the cowboys might raid other patriot homes.

In that year of 1782, the houses were widely scattered in the rural community of Monroe, New York. But the dauntless Phebe managed to make it to the nearest house before she collapsed. From there, the alarm was carried by others from farm to farm, until a full company of men had been organized to go after the outlaws.

By the time Phebe had recovered, all of the outlaws—including the vicious Benjamin Kelley—were either dead or awaiting trial. Meanwhile, the people of Monroe were tending to the Reynolds family, the men doing the necessary farm chores, the women taking care of the house and the newborn daughter, Polly.

For many weeks there were daily visits by various doctors who lived in the community. Yet when their fees were offered to them, each man shook his head. Turning to Phebe, they filled her hands with coins from their own pockets. After all, they explained, it was Phebe who had saved her family and warned the community—and it was to Phebe they owed a debt of courage.

WHAT CAN BE SEEN TODAY

NEW YORK: After her marriage to Jeremiah Drake, Phebe Reynolds lived in Neversink, in Sullivan County, New York. She is buried in the Pound Cemetery there, where a small white marble slab marks her grave. Nearby a granite spire over her parents' graves makes brief mention of the cowboy raid. (The Pound Cemetery is about a mile from Route 55 on Myers Road in Neversink. It may be visited at any time.)

Betty Zane

120 YARDS OF TERROR

"Not much of a homecoming for you, is it?"

Betty Zane looked over at the girl who had just joined her in the blockhouse at Fort Henry. Then together they stared out at the Ohio River moving sluggishly along under the chicory-blue September sky. It all seemed so peaceful, so pastoral—except for the hundreds of Indians and British circling the fort.

"You really didn't have to invite so many guests!" Betty tried to joke, but the other girl didn't even smile.

"If I'd been sent to school in Philadelphia," she said, "I'd *never* come back here!"

"Well, we're both here," Betty stated flatly. "So we might just as well concentrate on defending the fort— or else Simon Girty will be here, too!"

As if in answer to his name, the notorious renegade

approached the fort under a flag of truce. His demands were simple: surrender or be massacred by the 350 men under his command.

There were fewer than sixty people within the stockade, forty of them women and children, but they answered Simon Girty with loud cries of "Never!"

"I'll give you some time to think about it," Girty shouted back, then spurred his horse away.

He returned at sunset to make the same demand.

"Stay right where you are, Girty," he was told. "That way, you'll be caught in the cross fire when our messenger returns with reinforcements!"

"Your messenger is dead!" Simon Girty bellowed.

An immediate hush fell over the people inside the fort. Then a shrewd old Indian fighter named Sullivan stepped up to the barricade. "If that's true," he challenged Girty, "then tell me what the messenger looked like!"

"Why . . . why, he . . ." the startled renegade sputtered. "He was young with fair features."

Betty Zane joined in the derisive laughter that echoed through the fort.

"Girty, you're a liar!" Sullivan shouted over the din. "The man we sent was old and gray. Now, why don't you pack up your Redcoats and redmen and get out of here while you can?"

The stalemated Girty thundered off. However, as

twilight gave way to dark, it was apparent that he had
no intention of giving up the siege.

"Well, at least we'll have a night's sleep before they
attack," someone ventured.

"I doubt that," Sullivan spoke up.

"But Indians don't attack at night."

"Don't try putting all Indians in the same wigwam,"
Sullivan advised tartly. "Some Indians have no qualms
about night fighting—and Girty's are that kind."

There was a chorus of fearful murmurs, which caused
Sullivan to hurriedly add, "But we'll be able to hold out
until help comes. Don't worry about that!"

Nor was there any panic throughout the long night.
Girty's men did attack, but the walls of Fort Henry
were strong and its eighteen men strategically placed.
Thus, with the women loading and cooling the rifles, as
well as casting bullets, they greeted the dawn without
mishap or massacre.

Girty continued his attack throughout the day, but at
no time did the fort's defenders show any sign of weakening. There was a weakness, however, which was discovered later that afternoon. The fort was running out
of gunpowder!

Betty Zane was quick to report that her brother, Colonel Ebenezer Zane, had a supply of powder in his
house. There was only one problem: the Zane cabin
stood at least sixty yards away from the fort!

Despite the fact that it would be suicide for any of them to step outside the fort, all the men volunteered to try for the power. They were in the midst of deciding on which one would go, when Betty Zane's voice rang out, "Not one of you men can be spared here. Nor do any of you know where the powder is hidden. I do, so I'll go!"

When none of the men would agree to this, Betty turned to Mr. Sullivan. "Isn't it true that Indians are as curious as children?"

When the old Indian fighter nodded, Betty went on, "They would surely shoot any man who went racing out of the gate, but what if . . ." She paused to make sure she had their attention. "What if a lone and unarmed girl were to stroll out in the direction of the cabin? Mightn't they be apt to hold their fire until they found out what she was doing?"

The men continued to argue against it, but they could not deny that there was a better chance of success with Betty's plan than with theirs.

When the gate of Fort Henry finally swung open, it was to permit a slim, dark-haired girl to leave. The Indians watched in amazement as she headed toward one of the outlying cabins, on what seemed to be an afternoon stroll.

Fortunately, they could not see her trembling hands or hear her wildly thudding heart—or know the sheer willpower it took to restrict her feet to that agonizingly slow pace.

Ten yards, twenty . . . then when she was halfway to the cabin, a series of wild whoops almost made her stumble. This was followed by a cacophony of nerve-severing dog-yelps. No longer was it curiosity that held the Indians in check—it was fear of a possible trap. And their piercing cries were calculated to shatter the composure of the steadily advancing girl.

But Betty Zane plodded on, as if deaf.

Her legs were aching as if she had covered a hundred miles instead of only sixty yards, but the cabin door was now only a few feet away. Two more steps and she was inside. She had made it!

Betty's feeling of triumph vanished, though, when another thought seared through her mind: *she still had to go back!*

The same trick would not work again—this she knew. What then? "Run like the devil is after me, that's what!" she murmured, as she found the gunpowder and tied it in a tablecloth.

She was almost to the door when she thought of something else. With a quick motion, she whipped her skirt over her head. Those prim schoolteachers in Philadelphia would surely "Tut! Tut!" over this, she smiled grimly. But they had never tried to outrun an Indian!

Now that she had rid herself of the impeding skirt, Betty hoisted the heavy bundle. Then taking three deep breaths, she sped out of the house.

For a few seconds, she was the only moving thing in sight. Then, like partridges flushed from the bushes, Indians appeared everywhere, racing to intercept her before she could reach the fort.

Meanwhile, bullets scissored through the grass all around her. What if one of them hit the gunpowder?

Gripping the knot of the tablecloth even more fiercely, Betty concentrated on the gate of the fort, now less than twenty yards away. Why wasn't it open? Didn't they see her coming?

Just as she thought she would surely ram into it, the gate swung open and she raced through. Those waiting inside were even more breathless than she was, but they managed a rousing shout of praise for the girl who had outwitted—and then outran—the best of Girty's marauders.

Simon Girty also heard the triumphant shout and realized that it must have been gunpowder the girl had carried into the fort. The significance of this daring act was only too apparent to the renegade. The people would never give up now, for not only had their powder supply been renewed, but their courage as well.

Before the sun had gone down the following day,

Simon Girty called off his siege and rode away from the frontier settlement that later grew into the city of Wheeling, West Virginia.

WHAT CAN BE SEEN TODAY

WEST VIRGINIA: The heroic deed of Betty Zane is commemorated on a marker located at 12th and Chapline streets (site of Fort Henry) in Wheeling, West Virginia.

OHIO: A statue of the heroine can be found in the Walnut Grove Cemetery in Martins Ferry.

Rebecca and Abigail Bates

THE ARMY OF TWO

Becky Bates shielded her blue eyes as she gazed across the harbor. In the distance the town of Scituate, Massachusetts, lay sparkling in the September sun.

"I still don't understand why we couldn't go along too!" Becky declared.

"Someone had to stay behind to help Mother," her sister Abigail pointed out.

"But Mother said she didn't need any help!" Becky stamped her foot, though it made no sound in the coarse sand of Cedar Point.

"Well, what if Father doesn't return from town before sunset? Someone must be here to start the beacon in the lighthouse," Abigail reminded her. "Then there's always the chance that the British . . ."

Both girls stared again at the quiet waters of Scituate

Harbor. There was no wreckage there now, but they would never forget what it had looked like on June 11, 1814. That was the terrible day three months ago when the British had raided Scituate. By the time the Redcoats sailed away, the harbor had been turned into an inferno of burning ships.

"The British wouldn't dare come back," Becky stated boldly. "Not since our soldiers have been stationed here at the lighthouse."

"But the soldiers aren't here today," Abigail was quick to say. "And neither is Father."

An uneasy feeling gripped Becky. Abigail was right. The American troops, restless after months of idleness, had begun to spend their days across the harbor in Scituate. The girls' father was unhappy over the careless attitude of the regiment, but there was little he could do about it. He was only the lighthouse keeper and had no authority over the soldiers.

Becky sighed as she turned back to the lighthouse. "Well, we might as well go see if there isn't some way we can help Mother, after all."

The long, narrow arm of land that was called Cedar Point curved around to protect the harbor of Scituate. Because of this, the girls did not get a glimpse of the blue-gray waters of the Atlantic Ocean until they had almost reached the lighthouse.

"A frigate! It's a British frigate!"

Abigail's cry made Becky's heart lurch, and she strained her eyes to identify the vessel fast approaching the harbor. Suddenly the wind caught the flag at the peak of the mast, unfurling it to full length. It was the fearsome British Union Jack!

Legs churning in the sand, the two girls raced for the lighthouse. "Mother! Mother, it's the British. They're coming again!"

By the time they reached the door, Mrs. Bates had opened it and the girls hurried inside.

"We must alert the regiment!" Mrs. Bates cried. "We must warn the people!" Quickly untying her apron, she took her bonnet from a peg near the door, and the three of them hurried outside.

But it was too late. The British frigate had already dropped anchor and launched two barges full of soldiers.

"There is no way to warn the people in Scituate now," Mrs. Bates said gloomily. "The British would see us if we tried to row the dory across the harbor. And it would take too long to go the roundabout way by land. I think it best that we hide ourselves among the cedars and sand dunes."

So saying, she began to walk away from the lighthouse. Then sensing that her two daughters were not following, she turned abruptly, an impatient look on her face.

Abigail was tugging at her sister's sleeve. But Becky only stood there, staring at the oncoming barges. "Hide

ourselves," she was murmuring. "So the British won't
see us . . ."

Then she shouted, "That's it! The British can't see
us among the dunes! Come on, Abigail!"

Abigail could only stare in amazement as Becky
darted back into the lighthouse. Then Abigail turned
to call, "Go ahead, Mother. I'll fetch Becky."

When Abigail stepped over the threshold, Becky was
struggling to lift a heavy drum the American soldiers
had left behind. "Help me, Abigail," she pleaded. "But
first get the fife over there. Papa taught me how to play
'Yankee Doodle,' remember?"

Abigail shook her head in bewildered agitation. "Of
course I remember," she said. "But what has 'Yankee
Doodle' got to do with this? As for the drum, there's
no time to save it. Come on, Becky. The British will be
landing at any minute. We must get to the dunes!"

"Indeed we must," Becky agreed. "But the drum and
the fife must go too!"

Fully convinced that her older sister had lost her
senses from fright, Abigail decided to humor her. "All
right, Becky. If you insist on having the drum and fife,
we'll take them along—only hurry!"

When the girls arrived behind the sand dune where
their mother waited, Becky breathlessly explained what
she had in mind. She paused only to hand the drum-
sticks to Abigail, then put the wooden fife to her lips.

Meanwhile, the British soldiers stirred restlessly in the barges, their eyes intent on the rocky beach that sloped up to the lighthouse. Not a word was said as they nervously clutched their guns.

Suddenly the silence was shattered by the staccato tapping of a drum. The Redcoats jerked to attention, straining to make out the pattern of the drumbeats.

Just as the soldiers turned apprehensive eyes to the officer in charge, the shrill voice of a fife joined the thump of the drum. It took only a few notes for them to recognize the detested American tune "Yankee Doodle."

The British commander aboard the frigate also heard the strident warning of the fife and drum. He had counted on surprising the Americans, for his landing party was not a large one. But now there would be no surprise. Nor was there any way of telling how many Americans might be waiting for them behind the dunes.

Within seconds, the commander's decision was made. He signaled the barges to return to the frigate.

Behind a sand dune on shore, a dark head popped up and a pair of blue eyes grew wide with delight.

"Hurrah!" came a triumphant shout.

But the British did not hear it. With the landing party safely back on board, they had hoisted sail and were fast making for the open Atlantic. Nor did they spot the two young girls joyously dancing around a dark red drum on shore.

Only later did the British commander of the frigate *La Hogue* find out that he had been frightened away by a pair of heroic teen-age sisters, who would forever afterward be proudly remembered as the "Army of Two."

WHAT CAN BE SEEN TODAY

MASSACHUSETTS: The sisters who made up the "Army of Two" are well remembered in the town they saved from British attack. The wooden fife played by Rebecca can be seen in the Scituate Lighthouse (located near the junction of Abigail, Rebecca, and Bates roads on Lighthouse Point), which is open on certain days in the summer. The Bates home on Beaver Dam and Jericho Road in Scituate (pronounced "Sit-you-it") is not open to visitors, but may be viewed from the outside. For specific days when the lighthouse is open, contact the Scituate Historical Society, Cudworth House (also open to the public), First Parish Road and Cudworth Road, Scituate, Massachusetts 02060.

Mary Pickersgill

"A FLAG THE BRITISH CAN SEE"

It was September and the time of harvest. Everywhere in Baltimore, housewives were busy preparing for the long winter months when the land produced few of its nourishing gifts.

It was the time when cucumbers had to be set in great barrels of brine for savory pickles. Apples and other fruit must be sliced, then dried on long strings. Root cellars were gradually being filled with bushels of potatoes and other tubers, while bulbous bouquets of browning onions were suspended from wooden poles.

Certain medicinal plants could be gathered only at this time of year, such as the purple berries of the pokeweed and the roots of the green hellebore. Then there were the herbs and spices—rosemary, fennel, parsley, and dill, to name only a few—to be hung in bundles until the kitchen resembled a vast aromatic garden of drying plants.

This year of 1814 it was even more important than ever to lay in an abundant supply. For the British had singled out Baltimore as their next objective, swearing to overrun "that nest of hornets at the head of the Chesapeake."

Mary Pickersgill was even busier than most housewives that early September day. As a widow, she not only had her many duties at home, but also made her living as a seamstress specializing in "ships' and military colors." Yet she readily left her work table when her daughter Caroline came into the kitchen to say there were unexpected visitors at the front door.

Sending Caroline to let them in, Mary took off her apron and straightened the white ruffled morning cap she wore. Then she went into the parlor to find the callers were none other than Commodore Joshua Barney and Brigadier General John Strickler.

The general came right to the point. As everyone knew, the British were determined to capture Baltimore. To do this, they would sail up Chesapeake Bay and into the Potapsco River. There they would face the guns of Fort McHenry, which protected the city on the water's edge.

"We have equipped the fort for the impending attack," Strickler told Mary. "But we forgot one thing. We need . . ."

"A flag!" Commodore Barney broke in. "The British will attack any day, and we must have a flag to fly over the fort."

General Strickler nodded forcefully. "A flag those British devils can see from far down in Chesapeake Bay!"

"A flag that they will understand means no surrender!" Barney concluded.

For a moment Mary was silent. Perhaps she was thinking of the many and important household chores that would be left undone if she accepted this assignment. More likely, she was remembering that it was her own mother, Rebecca Young, who had been commissioned by George Washington to make the first banner of the Revolution, called the "Grand Union Flag."

For this reason, if no other, there was only one answer Mary could give, "I'll make the biggest and best flag I possibly can—and as fast as I can."

Fourteen-year-old Caroline Pickersgill was listening as Commodore Barney and General Strickler gave her mother the dimensions of the flag. As soon as the military men left the small house on Pratt Street, the girl burst out, "But we don't have enough room here to make such a giant banner!"

What Caroline said was only too true, Mary realized.

None of the rooms in her house was large enough for the undertaking. But defeat had no place in Mary's nature, and with a cheerful smile she answered, "We'll manage somehow."

Mary Pickersgill did manage. First she found an empty malt house nearby where the huge banner could be laid out flat. Then enlisting the aid of her mother, her two nieces, and Caroline, Mary set to work.

Over four hundred yards of hand-woven wool bunting would be needed to make a flag that measured thirty feet wide by forty-two feet long. Each stitch had to be sewn by hand, each of the fifteen white stars set carefully on their field of blue. Such a flag would take months to make—but Mary had less than two weeks.

Often Caroline would find her mother still working long after midnight, her eyes red-rimmed from exhaustion and candle smoke. But she would not listen to the pleas of her daughter to get some rest. "The flag must be ready," she would say, and continue pushing her needle in and out of the heavy bunting.

Finally the flag was completed, and not a day too soon. At 5:46 on the morning of September 13, 1814, a fleet of sixteen British warships opened fire on Fort McHenry.

On board a truce ship anchored in the Potapsco River was a young lawyer from Washington. He had been negotiating for the release of his friend, Dr. Beanes, who

had been captured by the British. Admiral Cochrane had agreed to free the prisoner, but only after the bombardment of Fort McHenry was over. Therefore, the lawyer was forced to remain on board the truce ship as the enemy lobbed shell after shell at the fortress protecting Baltimore.

All day long and throughout the night the American lawyer watched, thrilling each time a shell-burst lighted the sky enough for him to see that his country's banner still flew from the ramparts of the fort. And as he watched, he composed a poem on the back of an old letter he had in his pocket.

At dawn on September 14, 1814, the shell-pierced but unconquered banner still challenged the British, who finally gave up and sailed away. Meanwhile, the young lawyer, who had been released from the truce ship, returned to his Baltimore hotel room. There he rewrote his poem, which he called "The Defense of Fort McHenry."

A week later the poem was printed in the Baltimore *Patriot*, and before long it was set to music and sung as a song.

Today people the world over know this poem as "The Star-Spangled Banner"—the national anthem Francis Scott Key wrote while watching the flag Mary Pickersgill had made large enough for the British to see, and strong enough that no enemy shell could tear it from its staff. The flag that would forever afterward represent "the land of the free and the home of the brave."

WHAT CAN BE SEEN TODAY

MARYLAND: The home of Mary Pickersgill, now called the Star-Spangled Banner Flag House, stands at 844 East Pratt Street (corner of Albermarle Street) in Baltimore. The Flag House and the adjacent 1812 War Military Museum are open to the public every day except Monday.

Fort McHenry (at the end of East Fort Avenue in Baltimore) is now a National Monument and Historic Shrine. It is open seven days a week from late June through Labor Day.

WASHINGTON, D.C.: The Star-Spangled Banner which flew over Fort McHenry during the bombardment is on display on the second floor of the Smithsonian Institution's Museum of History and Technology, located at 14th Street and Constitution Avenue. The museum is open every day of the year, except for Christmas.

. . . And All the Others

The heroines whose stories have been told in the preceding chapters represent only a small percentage of the women and girls who risked their lives to establish these United States during the critical four decades spanning 1774 to 1814.

Unfortunately, the names and exploits of many of these heroines have been lost or forgotten in the passage of time. In other cases, only a brief mention can be found. For instance, there is a story about a girl who lived near Williamsbridge in what is now the borough of the Bronx in New York City.

One day in 1777, a band of Americans was about to march into an ambush, when this young girl spotted the waiting Tories. Though aware she was making a target of herself, the girl bravely signaled the approaching Americans from an upper-story window of her house, thereby saving them from the trap. Her name is not recorded—only the selfless deed which saved so many American lives that day.

As for the heroines whose names and stories are both still remembered, there is not enough room in this book to list them all. However, the following assortment of mini-biographies will help to round out the picture of the numerous women who served their country so well and in so many different ways.

Hannah Arnett

During the early days of the Revolution, when it seemed the Americans had no chance of winning, the British hoped to avoid further bloodshed by offering pardons to the rebels if they would swear allegiance to the King. This was seriously considered by many Americans, particularly those in New York and New Jersey, which had felt the full brunt of the war up to that time.

In December, 1776, a group of patriots met in the Elizabethtown, New Jersey, home of Isaac Arnett. There they decided to accept the pardon—that is, until Hannah Arnett confronted them.

Following a forceful argument that would have done

justice to Thomas Paine himself, Mrs. Arnett then issued a fervent plea that they continue to fight for American independence. When she was through, she had won over every single man in the room, and not one of them accepted the British pardon.

Ann Clay

Although her husband Joseph is better known to historians, Ann Clay is still remembered for the dedication she displayed in 1780 while tending the American wounded after the disastrous Battle of Camden in South Carolina.

Polly Cooper

Throughout the Revolutionary War, an Oneida Indian woman named Polly Cooper served as George Washington's cook and housekeeper. Though the war lasted for seven years, Polly refused to accept any pay for her services, insisting that it was her patriotic duty. Congress later recognized this unselfish Indian woman's contribution by allocating money for a magnificent shawl which was presented to Polly as a gift of the United States.

Lucretia Emmons

When a party of about sixty Tories surrounded the house of Captain Joshua Huddy in Monmouth County,

New Jersey, the only one there to help him was a servant girl named Lucretia Emmons. Though she could have easily slipped away before the fighting started, this courageous, twenty-year-old black girl chose to remain. Lucretia loaded the guns while Huddy ran from window to window, firing out at the attackers.

Convinced there were more than just two people defending the house, the Tories abandoned their plan to overrun it. But they did not give up, and decided to set fire to the house. By that time, however, the noise had aroused the neighborhood and a rescue party of Huddy's men arrived soon afterward.

Jemima Johnson

On August 15, 1782, a band of six hundred Indians, British, and Canadians surrounded the stockade of Bryan's Station near Lexington, Kentucky. With little advance warning, the settlers had no time to lay in a supply of water from the creek outside the stockade. Yet as the hot day wore on, it was only too obvious that they would never survive a siege without water.

The following morning, Jemima Johnson came up with a daring plan to lead a party of women to the creek. Acting as if they were unaware of the surrounding enemy, the group of twelve women and sixteen girls left through the back door of the stockade, while the men stood guard with their guns. The ruse worked and the water-carriers returned safely, allowing the inhabitants of Bryan's Station to hold out until help arrived from Lexington.

Mammy Kate

On Valentine's Day in 1779, Stephen Heard was captured by the British during the Battle of Kettle Creek in Georgia. Since there was already a price on his head, Heard was sentenced to be executed. However, on the day before he was to die, a courageous servant woman, known only as Mammy Kate, rescued Heard, who later became Governor of Georgia.

Anna Maria Lane

If it were not for Governor William H. Cabell of Virginia, even the little bit known about Anna Maria Lane might have been forgotten. In a message to the Virginia Legislature during its 1807–1808 session, the Governor asked that some financial consideration be given to Anna Maria Lane, who was then working as a nurse in the soldiers' barracks near Richmond. The reason he gave was that:

Anna Maria Lane is very infirm, having been disabled by a severe wound, which she received while fighting as a common soldier in one of our Revolutionary battles, from which she never has recovered, and perhaps never will recover.

The legislature promptly responded by granting her a pension on the grounds that she "in the garb and with the courage of a soldier performed extraordinary military services and received a severe wound at the Battle of Germantown" in Pennsylvania.

Whatever those services were is not known, but they must have been extraordinary indeed. For Anna Maria was awarded $100 a year, whereas the average soldier's pension was only $40.

Nonhelema

Known as the "Grenadier Squaw" because of her proud bearing and height, Nonhelema remained friendly with the patriots of Fort Randolph, West Virginia, even after her brother, Shawnee Chief Cornstalk, was brutally murdered in 1777.

The following May, Fort Randolph was besieged by a band of Indians, who gave up after a week and moved on. Knowing that other settlements in the war party's path must be warned, Nonhelema disguised two white men as Indians. Her work was so good that the men were able to pass among the marauding Indians on the trail without being detected. Then they rode on to warn the people near Donnally's Fort of the Indians' approach.

Faith Trumbull

Few people have not heard about the desperate plight of the American forces at Valley Forge during the winter of 1777–1778. All over the colonies collections were taken up for the starving and freezing soldiers. When one was made at the Meeting House in Lebanon, Connecticut, Faith Trumbull wanted to inspire the other members of the congregation to give as much as they could. Therefore, she donated a handsome cloak that had been given to her by the French General Rochambeau. (Rochambeau later joined the Continental Army.)

The example of the expensive cloak given so unselfishly had the effect Mrs. Trumbull hoped for, and a large collection was made that day. As for her cloak, it was cut up to make trimming for uniforms.

Jinnie Waglum

When George Washington was planning to march his army from Trenton to Princeton, New Jersey, he could not find any scout who knew the country well enough to avoid the major highways. Since the British were watching those main roads, Washington was in a dangerous predicament until a local woman named Jinnie Waglum offered her services.

Donning a soldier's hat and coat, Mrs. Waglum proudly guided the army over byroads to Princeton. There on January 3, 1777, in a surprising upset victory, Washington drove the enemy back toward New Brunswick.

Peggy Warne

At a time when most doctors were away at war, Margaret ("Aunt Peggy") Warne supplied the medical needs of civilians and soldiers alike. At first she practiced only in her immediate neighborhood of what is now Warren County, New Jersey. Then as word of her skill and dedication spread, her services were sought by people in outlying districts.

Whether day or night, "Aunt Peggy" would answer the call of the sick or wounded, riding horseback through all kinds of weather and terrain. Even after the war was over and her soldier husband returned home, she continued to act as nurse, midwife, and doctor, so that in time her name became a legend, later immortalized in W. Clement Moore's poem, "The Florence Nightingale of New Jersey."

WHAT CAN BE SEEN TODAY

Hannah Arnett

NEW JERSEY: The house where Hannah Arnett made her plea to the faltering rebels stood on the site now occupied by the Elizabeth Carteret Hotel (next to the Second Presbyterian Church on East Jersey Street, about halfway down the block from Broad Street in Elizabeth, New Jersey). On the wall of the hotel is a plaque commemorating Mrs. Arnett. Nearby the Elizabeth Court House on Broad Street is the First Presbyterian Churchyard (open at all times) where a bronze tablet marks the grave of this patriot.

Ann Clay

GEORGIA: An historical marker in Colonial Park Cemetery in Savannah, Georgia, details the contributions of Ann and Joseph Clay, both of whom are buried here. (Clay was Deputy Paymaster General for the Southern Department of the Continental Army.) The entrance to the park (open every day) is at Oglethorpe Avenue and Abercorn Street.

Lucretia Emmons

NEW JERSEY: The site of the Huddy home which Lucretia Emmons helped to defend is located near the intersection of Route 34 and the Colts Neck-Freehold Road in New Jersey. It is across the road from the still-standing Colts Neck Inn that Joshua Huddy once operated. Farther south, at Huddy Park in Toms River, can be found a replica of the blockhouse (open most days of the week) where Lucretia's employer was later captured by the British.

Mammy Kate

GEORGIA: Southeast of Middleton, just off Route 72 in Heardmont, Georgia, lies the ten-acre park dedicated to the memory of Governor Stephen Heard. Mammy Kate is buried near him in the old family cemetery called "God's Acre" within the park. A highway marker mentioning her is located nearby.

Anna Maria Lane

PENNSYLVANIA: The name of this little-known heroine cannot be found on any of the numerous markers in the Germantown section of Philadelphia, Pennsylvania. However, visitors to the area will find the main battle monument (in Vernon Park on Germantown Avenue near Chelton) to be of interest. In addition, the Chew estate, "Cliveden" (6400 Germantown Avenue), where much of the battle took place, is now open to the public on weekdays. One can only wonder if the severely wounded Anna Maria was among the many injured left at the Boehm German Reformed Church (on Penllyn Pike in Blue Bell) when the American Army retreated from Germantown.

Nonhelema

WEST VIRGINIA: On Route 60, west of Lewisburg, West Virginia, there is a marker mentioning the "Grenadier Squaw." See also the listing for Point Pleasant (Fort Randolph) at the end of the chapter on Anne Bailey.

Faith Trumbull

CONNECTICUT: The original meeting house where Faith Trumbull donated her cloak was destroyed by a hurricane, but a replica has been built in its place on Route 207 in the center of Lebanon, Connecticut. The meetinghouse (containing panelling from the original) is open every day.

Jinnie Waglum

NEW JERSEY: No memorials to Jinnie Waglum have been found. However, the battle to which she led Washington's Army is now commemorated at Princeton Battlefield State Park on Route 583 at the southern edge of Princeton, New Jersey. (The park is open daily.)

Peggy Warne

NEW JERSEY: Aunt Peggy's farmhouse no longer stands on the old Warne property in New Jersey, but there still can be seen a small sandstone building (marked by a plaque) believed to be the place where she stored and prepared her medicinal herbs. (Go south on the Asbury Road from Broadway, then east on the country road branching off just past Pohatcong Creek. The herb house is a few hundred yards down this road on the right-hand side.)

There is also a room named in memory of Peggy Warne in the Old Barracks Museum on South Willow Street (one block north of the War Memorial) in Trenton, New Jersey. The museum is open year round.

Acknowledgments

One of the nicest things about writing *Patriots in Petticoats* has been the dedicated people it has been my pleasure to meet. Without their interest and assistance, it would have been impossible to complete my research.

Therefore, my thanks are offered to: Laura P. Abbott, Vermont Historical Society; Tom Agnew, Georgia Department of Natural Resources; Linda Anderson, Kentucky Historical Society; William J. Artrip, Mason County (W. Va.) Historical Society; A.K. Baragwanath, Museum of the City of New York; Barbara M. Bauer, Montgomery County (Pa.) Tourist Bureau; Elizabeth Boggs, Pendleton County (W. Va.) Historical Society; Joseph Bresnan, New York City Parks, Recreation and Cultural Affairs Administration; Charles H. Bricknell, Plympton (Mass.) historian; Donna Christian,

Metropolitan Museum of Art; Shanna Columbus, Harrodsburg (Ky.) Bicentennial Committee; Richard Dale, Watoga State Park.

Also, Elsalyn Drucker, Monmouth County (N.J.) Historical Society; John P. Dumville, Royalton (Vt.) Historical Society; Barbara Eaton, Hart County (Ga.) Chamber of Commerce; Ray Fadden, Six Nations Indian Museum; Irma W. Franklin, Putnam County (N.Y.) Historical Society; Thomas P. Garigan, West Point Museum; Pauline Harman, Pendleton County (W. Va.) Historical Society; Annie Harrison, Kentucky Department of Libraries; Hilda Hoffman, Bucks County (Pa.) Historical-Tourist Commission; Emma Holtkamp, Boxwood Hall (N.J.); Mabel E. Irlé, Germantown Historical Society; Susanne King, American Revolution Bicentennial Commission of Connecticut; Donald E. Kloster, Smithsonian Institution; Andrew Kreinik, West Virginia American Revolution Bicentennial Commission; Kathleen Laidlaw, Scituate (Mass.) Historical Society; Alyce E. Lane, Old Barracks Association; Mary C. Lempenau, National Society Daughters of the American Revolution; Marjorie Lindsey, North Carolina Department of Cultural Resources.

In addition: Ernest A. Lucci, Massachusetts Department of Commerce and Development; Kathy McCormack, Sullivan County (N.Y.) Publicity and Tourism Department; Dorothy H. McGee, Town of Oyster Bay

American Revolution Bicentennial Commission; Lou Delle McIntosh, Kentucky Department of Parks; Harold R. Manakee, Maryland Historical Society; Mary-Paulding Martin, Star Spangled Banner Flag House Association; Mary K. Meyer, Maryland Historical Society; Allan L. Montgomery, Valley Forge State Park; Pauline Moody, Sharon, Mass.; James E. Mooney, Historical Society of Pennsylvania; Elizabeth V. Moore, Historic Edenton Association; Mary Jane Rankin, Virginia State Travel Service; T. Roth, Historical Society of Pennsylvania; Parke Rouse, Jr., Virginia Independence Bicentennial Commission; Ruth P. Schaffer, Philadelphia Convention and Visitors Bureau; William G. Smith, Sullivan County (N.Y.) Historical Society; Natalie Spassky, Metropolitan Museum of Art.

Finally: Bruce W. Stewart, Morristown (N.J.) National Historical Park; Keith D. Strawn, North Carolina Museum of History; Jaime Suits, New York State Library; Ray Thompson, Bicentennial Press; Celestina Ucciferri, Brooklyn Museum; Delbert Van Etten, Liberty Village (N.Y.) Historian; Mary M. Watt, Richmond Newspapers, Inc.; Jessica M. Weber, *Guideposts*; Pat Weibezahl, Peggy Warne Chapter, Daughters of the American Revolution; Waverly K. Winfree, Virginia Historical Society; Deborah Young and Carolyn J. Zinn, West Virginia Department of Archives and History.

If I have neglected to mention anyone who was kind

enough to help me, it is due to an inadvertent omission rather than inappreciation.

Thanks are also extended to Robert E. Frank in whose *Modern Woodmen Magazine* my earlier versions of the stories of Sybil Ludington, Tempe Wick, and the Bates sisters have appeared.

Last—but always first in my thoughts—my appreciation to my family for assisting me in so many ways, and most especially to my oldest son Stephen, who helped with the library "legwork."

Index

141

THE AUTHOR

Patricia Edwards Clyne was born in New York City and graduated from Hunter College with a B.A. in journalism. She worked as a reporter and also a free-lance editor.

Her love of history and exploring has taken her to numerous locations connected with the American Revolution and our country's struggle for independence, including many of the sites involving the heroines of *Patriots in Petticoats*.

Mrs. Clyne lives in New York with her husband and four sons. He is the author of numerous magazine articles and two previous children's books, *The Corduroy Road* and *Tunnels of Terror*.

THE ILLUSTRATOR

Richard Lebenson has been an illustrator of children's books for almost ten years. He received a B.F.A. and a master's degree from Pratt Institute.

Some of his more recent books, including *When the World's on Fire* and *Waiting for Mama*, also deal with historical subjects, which have been of particular interest to him throughout his career.

Mr. Lebenson has shown his etchings in a number of exhibits and galleries in New York City and abroad.